Grieve

Stories and Poems
about Grief and Loss

Volume 10

HUNTER
WRITERS
CENTRE

Grieve Volume 10
Hunter Writers Centre
PO BOX 494 The Junction
Newcastle NSW 2300

Email: publishing@hunterwriterscentre.org
Website: www.hunterwriterscentre.org

Grieve: Stories and Poems about Grief and Loss

ISBN 978-0-6488504-8-9

Cover design by HWC Publishing
Cover photos courtesy of iStock, Brett Nattrass, and Pollyana Ventura
Typesetting by HWC Publishing
2022 Published by Hunter Writers Centre Inc.

It's so much darker when a light goes out than it would have been if it had never shone
John Steinbeck

Foreword

Get with someone you can trust with tears, with anger, and wonderment and utter silence. Get that part done. The sooner the better. The only way around these things is through them.

This very matter-of-fact directive about dealing with grief comes from much lauded American poet and undertaker, Thomas Lynch. One might think a talented poet would find a more subtle and lyrical way to express himself on the matter. But isn't it true when we are mired in grief and loss, we would sometimes give anything to have someone tell us unequivocally what to do? In Lynch's day job, dealing with the dead and the loved ones left behind, he sees suffering constantly. And like all our wonderful Grieve sponsors: counsellors, palliative care workers, mental health practitioners and compassionate, emotional supporters, Lynch aims to help, even if it sometimes feels like medicine for us to hear. He has learned through the many years of witnessing grief, and experiencing his own, that the least effective way to move beyond the pain of loss is to ignore it.

That first statement of Lynch's made me think of what the Grieve anthology provides each year. Lynch, the poet, also understands the power of the human word to provide comfort, and to hold a mirror up to our own lives. Between these pages we find our 'someone' to trust with tears, anger, wonderment and the impossible complexities of loss and grief. The stories and poems become, in a small or large way, our guides and teachers, our colleagues and partners in the business of loss we might think we never signed up for. But we did, albeit without our consent. It is part of the small print of our human contract. We are destined to know grief in direct proportion with our capacity for love.

When I received the poetry entries, I expected to feel weighed down by the sheer size of the emotional content coming my way. But as I cried, and smiled, and felt my breath catch under my ribs, I knew at the heart of each of these pieces, the many faces of grief had a transformative beauty when passed through the fire of craft. The very best of the poems had built a crucible of words that held the unbearable heat of raw emotion. They were the most successful at using poetry's arcane power to transform base metal into gold.

You may find some of the subject matter in this anthology personally triggering. It was not a light decision for us to include those powerfully written pieces. We decided it would not be an authentic representation of the writers' experiences, nor our commitment to witness and validate, if we made our selection based on what would cause the least disturbance to the reader. Having said that, there are far more pieces that will gently shake your hand, than leave you shaken.

An immense thankyou to all the sponsors of this year's prize. Without you, the Grieve Awards could not exist. Congratulations to the winners, those who are anthologised, and to all this year's entrants who were courageous enough to put their innermost thoughts on paper.

Judy Johnson
Poetry Judge, 2022

Grieve 2022
10 Years

The Grieve project began as an activity only for members of Hunter Writers Centre. A decade ago, we held live readings throughout the year for our members and in August of that year—Grief Awareness month—we set the theme 'Grieve'. 85% of our members responded to the call for poems and stories. We were astounded. Had we stumbled on something here? Were people yearning to express their loss?

I called Trudy Hansen at the National Association of Loss and Grief and discussed extending the project across New South Wales. A decade later, I still remember her words at the time: 'Why not go national? Grief doesn't stop at the border.'

So, we took Grieve across Australia, believing it might run a year or two; that, once penned, everyone had had 'their say' about grief.

Hundreds of Australians responded. And, ten years later, the project is still running and we are thrilled to publish this 10th anniversary anthology.

Australians haven't finished telling their stories. We continue to be moved and educated and entertained by you, the writers. And the telling is always fresh.

There are as many ways to tell the experience of loss as there are people on this earth.

Karen Crofts
Director
Hunter Writers Centre

We acknowledge the Awabakal as the original custodians of the land on which this anthology was published.

Awards

The National Association of Loss and Grief (NALAG)
No Place for Flowers — Shereen Ricupero

The Pettigrew Family Funerals
Some Days the Air is Soft — Melanie Jansen

Palliative Care NSW
Climate Control — Mahli Rose

All About Grief
Outside Forever — Bronwyn Ryan

In Memory of Kenneth Davison
Waiting in Radiology — Richenda Rudman

Lake Macquarie Memorial Park
Cloudy Mountain — Tric O'Heare

Griefline
Heart Weeding — Deborah Huff-Horwood

Newcastle Memorial Park
The Nurse — Justine Kuszelyk

White Lady Funerals
My Father Teaches Me to Walk — Seetha Nambiar Dodd

Good Grief
Goodbye Girl — Kat S

Simplicity Funerals
The Day After We Buried You — Rose Lucas

David Lloyd Funerals (Newcastle & Hunter Valley)
Dear You — Kristen Roberts

Calvary Mater Newcastle
A Brother — Fiona Jarvis

In Memory of Trent Barden
Ashes to Gold - Jo Skinner

The Blue Knot Foundation
No Headstone — Em Readman

Mindframe
The Gift — Carolyn Eldridge-Alfonzetti

The Compassionate Friends
Passionfruit — Kylie Bates

Hunter New England Health, Mental Health Services
The Cull — David Campbell

In Memory of Kevin Corby
The Bally Wind — Louise Martin-Chew

World Award - nature or socio-political
The Taste of Bread — Mark Konik

World Award - nature or socio-political
After Fourteen Years, The Boorabbin Fire Finally Claims You
— Renee Schipp

No Place for Flowers

Shereen Ricupero

Flowers plume from the nest of my palms
thorns against flesh
as waves reach for my feet
with liquid stories.

Her ash melds with the tide
no earth, no stone
nowhere to press my fingers to her name
no place for flowers.

If I plunge my hands into the cold
lift them to my lips
let the ocean meander a path down
my arms, my chest, my belly
would she cling to the curves and hollows of my body?

Or is she gone and I'm here alone
visiting her where she is not
holding roses
standing in water
too salty to nourish them.

Some Days the Air is Soft

Melanie Jansen

'Look closely and you will see
Almost everyone carrying bags
Of cement on their shoulders'
    —Edward Hirsch, *Gabriel: A Poem*

Beep…click. The ICU staff entrance admits me, and I step
into taut air. Corridors are crowded: central line trolley,
a code blue pack; and bags of cement, waiting to be lifted up.

Grief is always in the air. Grief is Love's twin—her aching
reflection. Sadness suffuses her, floodlighting spaces Joy left
bare. Here we can feel lucky. Here, she belongs to others.

Some days the air is soft with her. She floats
in with each breath. Though she belongs
to others, she pays attention to us. It doesn't hurt

much when she takes her chisel and adds touches
to the lines on my face. Like when I hold a sweating
hand; when I press yet another needle into a small body.

Some days the air is thick with her. She sticks
to my clothes, insistent. She turns the atmosphere
to honey, and I walk with weights strapped

around my ankles. My mirror showed me three
grey hairs today, gifts from other people's children.
One was a great save. Beat the odds. Some days

she roils, and we hold her in all her shapes. Over years
she has taught me words. In time, schooled me in silence.
Some days she soaks through – she bruises, burns me.

Like when I lay a dead child in a parent's arms. Grief swathes
them in wretched splendour. She thieves breath, hurls pain.
We can only hold them, in this first of the infinite storms.

Climate Control

Mahli Rose

Her grief felt like a cliché. She certainly wasn't the first person to sit with her head in her hands on those godforsaken waiting room chairs, the artificial lighting glaring down at her. Everybody seemed to speak quietly in the ICU, like they were worried one sharp noise would push someone over the edge. Emmy stared at her shoelaces, noting that the right one was significantly more worn than the left. She heard the soft squeak on the polished floor that signalled the approaching nurse and managed to raise her head.

'It's time,' the nurse said, her eyes sympathetic. 'You can come in and say goodbye now.'

Emmy rose from the chair, feeling the rough fibres against her thighs. She had forgotten a jumper again and goosebumps decorated her arms. Outside, it was a humid thirty-three degrees, smack bang in the middle of summer. In here, the constant air conditioning ensured no one cracked a sweat. She walked down the corridor, passing rooms she had grown accustomed to over the past couple of weeks. She saw the rosary beads dangling from the hands of the elderly lady, who sat praying by her husband's bed during visiting hours each day. Emmy found herself resenting her, envious of her faith. Maybe it was all an act, a desperate attempt at finding some semblance of control. Probably not, though. Likely, she was a lifelong believer and speaking to her God was a regular occurrence. Emmy wondered whether it would pay off this time.

They reached the private room he had been given, courtesy of the hospital when there was nothing more they could do. Emmy stood by the bed, attempting to block out the beeping. The nurse touched her shoulder blade gently.

'I'll be just outside, let me know when you're ready.' She exited the room, allowing the door to gently close behind her.

Emmy turned to look at him. He looked deceivingly peaceful if you could pretend the tubes weren't there. His chest rose and fell like it did at home. She could picture it in the dawn light, the dark hairs soft against her skin. She was always a light sleeper, often waking with the first magpie.

This gave her the opportunity to watch him. Sometimes his eyes would flicker, or his mouth would twitch, the sign of a dream. She would grin and gently kiss his jaw, trying not to wake him but hopeful he would stir.

She couldn't remember the last time they had woken together. It must have been over a fortnight ago. Had it been the weekend, or a workday? Had he rolled over to spoon her, his hand finding hers? Or had he snuck out of bed, quietly making her a coffee and delivering it with a clink onto the bedside table?

She stared at his expressionless face, her mind blank. Then she turned to the door and called for the nurse.

13

Outside Forever

Bronwyn Ryan

We'd never been hiking before, never even seen the bush. As usual, Terry was a major pain.

I thought all little brothers were like Terry—forever screaming and jumping, always getting everyone's attention, even if I was dying! He was more than just annoying. Mum said Terry had a problem in his head.

I was really his only friend in the world.

He was OK I guess, especially when we played video games. They calmed him down. Mum tried hard to limit our gaming—it's unhealthy, apparently...Mum tried hard to do a lot for us boys.

'No inside games today boys, just good outside fun!'

We drove for hours up into the mountains. Naturally, Terry whinged the whole way. But when we got there, it was awesome. The air was different, sorta cold and sweet to swallow. The track looked lit too—like a game, only real.

Terry stood still for a bit, looking up, listening to the thousands of birds. Weird—he normally freaked out at new stuff.

'Stay together boys,' Mum yelled after us.

Terry'd run ahead, I'd catch him up and then we'd wait for Mum. After lunch, Terry and I peed under a tree—we cracked up! Mum said it was OK in the bush. The last time I saw Terry, he took off around a bend up the track.

The rest of that day is all mixed up in my head: Mum screaming, 'Terry!' for hours; police and people in hi-vis vests thrashing the bush; thundering choppers churning the trees; everyone looking for Terry.

'He'd hate all this noise,' I mumbled, but no one listened. It went on into the night, more men, more flashing lights, more noise. Mum came to check on me a few times, sobbing and frantic.

'Where'd he go, Pete? Think!'

And, 'Why didn't you stay with him?'

And in the pink dawn light, 'Oh Pete, where's our Terry?'

The birds were really quiet that morning.

Months passed. Mum said no to a funeral, he wasn't dead. She cried a lot, most days she couldn't get out of bed. I got pretty good in the kitchen.

And ugh, the counsellors—I hated the lady with red lipstick and purple glasses! She kept asking me about how annoying Terry was and how angry I'd felt with him. Was I jealous of all the attention Mum paid him? She kept asking me over and over about my feelings.

I still don't know the answer to that. I can't put it into proper words. Sometimes it's like when Matt punched me in the guts at school and I couldn't breathe properly. But I didn't tell her that—she'd probably think I punched Terry that day back in the bush.

He's fading and blurry now, like the baby photos Mum's always looking at. I try to imagine what he'd be like as an older kid, but I can't do it.

There's just so much I can't do since I lost Terry.

Waiting in Radiology

Richenda Rudman

The old man sits, the creases of his shirt cut sharp
by his wife whose hands are clasped in front;
by his wife who wears new stockings
with slip-on shoes, with slip-on skirt—
easy on, easy off.

The old man ponders his wife's hands;
they are rarely still, rarely stop,
and he sees for the first time,
the wedding ring resting in the pillow of her finger,
and he ponders for the first time, the indent it will leave behind.

Today his own fingers stall
while looping the laces of his shoes;
his breath catches, then begins again
to finish that which he has not given thought to
for such a long, long time.

The old couple arrive early
to this waiting room
and its dark squares of carpet, like sky, storm-filled,
and they listen for sounds of their name to be called
above a joke that is killing the newsreaders on morning tv.

In time, they are summoned
to a blue-curtained cubicle
from where the wife enters a lead-lined room,
where the inside of her is illuminated more than the saint she is named for
and she is baffled, but unquestioning, at the findings.

And the old man leaves slowly
down the grey corridor,
carrying his wife's bag
containing her mysteries,
carrying it for the second last time.

Cloudy Mountain[1]

Tric O'Heare

The time is coming to gift your silver flute
      to the Conservatorium.
Another young woman will play it
      erasing your fingerprints with her own
the first time she takes it up.
      She will lay her lip where yours had been
and her first confident breath
      will release a breath of yours that has lain there
in that cold hollow for two autumns.

The student, when she opens the black case
      will hardly glance at our tucked-in card
which describes your soul and love of music
      but when she flicks through your books
Cloudy Mountain will catch her eye
      so carefully annotated in your own hand
it reads like your testament to beauty
      and the worth in trying to get things right.

[1] *Cloudy Mountain*, a 1981 composition for flute and piano by Anne Boyd

Heart Weeding
Deborah Huff-Horwood

Her old heart is racing. Skipping.

'Not the ideal,' says their doctor, so she's sent for tests, and before they both know it, she's in hospital for surgery. Unable to visit, he is left, adrift.

Back home, alone, he's been trembling. So here he is, walking beside the lake. There's a breeze off it, chilling his neck, his hands clasped, mouth fixed. His only focus is on hope—and on his phone in his back pocket. Neither give him satisfaction.

When he reaches the wetlands he pulls his gloves from his jacket pocket, draws them over his gnarled fingers and rips into the weeds beside the boardwalk. Here he can lose time, mark time. He grasps and yanks, deposits and returns, and will keep it up until the piles on the path are big enough to bag. In his focus on the task—caring for his suburb as they've always done—he loses his trembling. But it's his heart being cut open too, and his wife's not here to suture him.

He pulls off his gloves to check his phone.

Pedestrians are coming, cyclists too. Spinning tyres whirl past and will slip if he doesn't bag these leaves and tendrils. From another pocket he pulls a much-used plastic bag. He shakes it loose and gathers large handfuls of weeds into it. Then he continues, facing the human traffic, dragging his bag as he goes.

What of his wife?

He drops his phone because he forgot to remove his gloves. He fumbles the unlock code, relieved the screen isn't cracked. This vacuum of her absence bites chillier than the day.

He rubs his lower back, surveys his work, brushes the dirt off the boardwalk with his boot and removes his gloves, rolling them and replacing them in his pocket. Billowing grey clouds roll in. Where's his wife's witty commentary on the weather?

Detouring via a hopper, he unties the knotted plastic, lifts it in one hand while levering the lid with his other and shakes it free. The weeds rain down, resounding on the metal, but now water rains too, and he has no umbrella. He deserves this: punishment for his good health. Something must have gone wrong for the hospital not to have called. He gives the bag a final shake, rolls it and replaces it small in his pocket. Stooping with the weight of absence, he sets his sights on home.

He's imagining her there. There's a book in her lap. A teacup beside her armchair. Sun is sloping through the windows. She'll delight at his arrival home.

Finally at his front door, he digs for his key. At the same time, he hears his phone. His wet hands almost drop it. His own heart is racing, skipping.

'Hello?'

The doctor talks, while he slumps against the doorframe.

An automaton, he pushes inside, shuts the door against the world, peels off his sodden jacket. He catches his expression in the hallway mirror. Adrift, and about to drown.

19

The Nurse

Justine Kuszelyk

I quietly placed his limp, tiny body in her arms. I helped her settle back into the couch and she positioned him on her lap so that she cradled his head in her hands, with his feet against her still swollen belly. She sighed. She gazed at his face, stroking his downy cheek, his nose. She leaned over and breathed him in.

I moved to the other side of the room in silence, busying myself with necessary paperwork but always watching, listening and taking my cues from her. In the subdued light of the hospital room, I could see the glisten of her quiet tears.

She raised him more upright, so his face was closer to hers. She kissed his cheeks, his eyes, his forehead. She began telling him the secrets in her heart. She told him of the life she had planned for them both, the favourite places they would have visited together, the people who would have loved him. She talked about their home, his bedroom and everything she'd prepared. She talked about their life, the two of them, and how they would have filled it with wonder and laughter and perfect moments of exquisiteness. She told him how they'd have laid in bed together on a Sunday morning, listening to the rain and reading stories. She said they'd have cooked pancakes, and danced and sang.

She spoke of all of her hopes for his future, the dreams she'd had of his birth, and his life. She told him that from the moment she knew he was growing within her she had loved him, and that she would always love him. Because she was his mummy, and she was so very glad that he'd come into her life and already taught her so much. She told him she was so sorry he couldn't stay.

I was rooted to the spot, by the desk lamp. I was writing updated notes, but really I was anchored to her, listening to her. I felt embarrassed, like I was intruding on the most intimate moment.

My Father Teaches Me to Walk

Seetha Nambiar Dodd

Your giant strides pave my way. Struggling to keep up, I skip a few steps. You look back to check I am there. *Swing your arms*, you say. *It helps*. More than a guide, you are the pacemaker on this course—setting the speed, always just out of reach.

There is a time, a short time, when we stroll side by side, see eye to eye. The future, giddy with promise, rolls out the red carpet and invites us to dream. We assume a clear path, blind to the warning signs. *Keep your back straight*, you say. *Good posture helps.*

When the cancer comes, it swaggers into your lungs, and suddenly I cannot breathe. When you're not looking, I stumble over emotions, fall at the simplest hurdles. You remain steadfast—side-stepping the pain, and the conversations. I never ask how you do it, never show you my trembling heart, or ask if yours might be trembling too. Instead, we carry on, in this strange limbo. By day, we tiptoe around our feelings. I spend my nights slow-dancing with regret. *Chin up*, your eyes say. *It helps*. I look away, afraid of what I might reveal.

Then you die, and I plod through grief, haul myself through tedious days. At inconvenient times, I lose my footing. The route ahead is both mountain and ravine—I am familiar with neither. I try to swing my arms, try to keep my back straight and my chin up, but nothing helps. Nothing helps.

It takes a while, a long while, but one day the view changes. In a quiet, ordinary moment, I hear you walking behind me. I know you are examining my path, noting my pace. I want to turn around. I long to look back. But I don't. I'm afraid you won't be there.

Then your voice floats across the years—a familiar tone that cuts through the heartache and the regret. *Keep moving*, you say. *Put one foot in front of the other. It helps.*

If I can hear you, perhaps you can hear me too. Maybe you always could. Still, it is time to say it:

Thank you for walking with me. I love you. I miss you.

Goodbye Girl

Kat S

Grief for someone still living seeps in slowly. Like stars gently appearing in a night darkened sky, the grief you brought to our door, my sweet girl, came surreptitiously, like self-harm. A stinging pain inflicted daily in a thousand tiny cuts upon the skin of my fierce love for you. A peculiar grief that is singular to all who walk that liminal shadowed space beside desperate children.

We watch the slow hollowing out of the plump cheeked, wild and smiling child you once were. We mourn the soundless cessation of connection. We take the verbal blows, reel back from slamming doors. Sob with anger and despair as you carve your confusion out in long bitter lines, a ragged red map of unhappiness. We offer whatever small measure of love is acceptable to this new person bursting out of the old. We crop long golden hair to the scalp. We stand beside you as a deeper truth ends one life and begins another.

I tenderly hold the grief of a gender rejected, a daughter lost. I feel it as an umbilical tug, a gut-wrenching splitting apart. I wake up in the small hours with the cold thrill of anxiety, creeping down to your room in the thick darkness to check, as I once did when you were brand new, that your chest still rises and falls with sleep, that your eyes are only closed in troubled repose, not forever closed by your own hand.

I drown all dreams of who I believed you might be. I take down photographs that celebrate you as a mischievous glowing girl, a climber of trees, a lover of all small, injured and displaced creatures. I make room for the young man you are slowly becoming. A face filled now with piercings instead of smiles. And I accept that a grief such as this has no end in sight. Each day full of questions that I cannot answer, rebuffs I find hard to weather, caustic words that wound this tender heart. Like a teen in love, I invent excuses to be with you. I bring freshly laundered clothes that are too big for your skinny frame; pills to lighten the dark cloud, others to numb the grief you too must ride out. I bring books which might help but don't, lying unread on your bedside table because this new path you stomp has sapped you of all your previously loved pursuits and left you far away and empty.

Yet even grief contains hope. I lean into tiny moments of connection and a hope for a future where your dad and I are once again allowed to reach out and gently stroke that much loved face, pull you into an embrace that speaks of safety and love beyond gender, that offers a new slate for you to write yourself upon, so that we may read the story of you and you may know yourself truly, deeply, madly loved. Always and in all ways.

The Day After We Buried You

Rose Lucas

saturday continues   apparently unperturbed and
relentless   into sunday   and in this widening
ribbon of time   we have continued
to walk   make dinner   to hold

each other in the
quiet of turning sheets then

waking into morning's cool spill
all the while knowing
that you are
still   lying where we placed you

your furred body   its gold miasma that floated
gossamer   into many days

already loosened
muscle from bone   organ from organ—
first we cradled you
re-telling your stories   weeping and

smiling into our teacups
until   fold by fold   we wrapped you

our small   unmoving   parcel of love
in the clarity of cotton

making a space in the garden   small
as you liked it   swaddled close

and sheltered   below the laden arms
of the lemon tree

tuck of paws   the sweetness of your inclined head
listening   while soil trickles   grain by grain
covering your old bones   and holding you
all through this night's long passage

this tender place where one thing   must finally
unravel   into the possibility of another

Dear You

Kristen Roberts

The corellas are preaching their missives
to a vacant sky, the sun most ways
to a different day, a foreign dawn.
I can't keep the grass from the driveway
but there's still only weed in the lawn.

I'm keeping the bellies of roos full of new grevilleas
while rabbits expose the roots of other plantings
like untested prophecies. There hasn't been a day yet
where I feel like I'm winning at this.

The cat still prefers water from the shower floor
(I've read it's to do with the taste of minerals)
and your chair is his permanent morning spot.
An autumn squall brought down countless boughs
and snapped a sapling gum in two,
that flowering favourite towards the dam.
I nursed it for months,
murmured to it and stroked its slender trunk
and it just sent out new leaves beneath the point of trauma.
I, as yet, have not.

I have taken to wearing only earrings you gave me
and keep my hair up in a knot.
Two girls no more than twelve
walk a dog past here most afternoons—
one always has her hair in a braid,
neat and tight like ribs against her skull,
rows of bones of hair. It seems a naïve sense of control;
she'll find out soon enough.

Bushfires have raged through the coastal towns
we once escaped to, so extreme that distant cities choked
on the smoke of others' tragedies, everyone's tragedy.
I know *we* always treated this land like our lung

but I've come to realise that so too is happiness—
grief is a bellows of inadequate air,
and I fear it will always be hard to breathe without you.

A Brother

Fiona Jarvis

From his hospital bed, the man calls the sister he hasn't seen for twenty years to tell her he is dying. The pain in her voice shocks him. He shouldn't have called.

'I'll fly up,' she says.

'Don't. What's the point?'

She comes anyway, the stains of her tears are on her cheeks and in her shaky smile as she enters his room. He watches her, wary, seeing traces of his own face in hers. What will she expect of him? He braces himself, but his sister surprises and pleases him. She doesn't launch herself at him, cling to him. She is purposeful, pragmatic, takes stock of his surrounds, plugs in his laptop and fills his waxed paper cup with water from the plastic jug.

She visits his home each day and follows his directions that lead her to the papers she will need to account for, to cancel his life's activities once he has gone. She doesn't ask about the squalor in his house. She weeps and is immeasurably tender as she uses her hands to show him how she held his elderly cat as it was euthanised, an act of mercy he requested. He saves his own tears for his furry companion until after his sister has left his room.

'I'll see you soon,' his sister says to him a week and one day later. Her brows flick up and she grins. Her brother will soon be strong enough to leave hospital, according to his doctor. She has plans for him.

'Come home to us,' she says. 'I'll get everything ready.' She touches his cheek with her hand. How good it feels to have someone else's skin against his own. She leans over, kisses his forehead and steps back.

'You'll be fine.'

'Bye,' he lifts an arm. His sister blows him a kiss. His bowels gurgle. Loose, ready again. There's pain with it now. I won't be coming home, he should tell her, but doesn't. His sister opens and closes her fingers in a wave, smiles, turns, and leaves.

He thinks of his sister as he watches the young nurse trying to contain the mess in the plastic nappy she has pulled down his emaciated legs. This is the second, third, possibly fourth incident of the day. She doesn't look at him or speak. Could she possibly be as disgusted with him as he is?

His evening meal arrives. The man rejects the tray coming towards him. How enormous his hands look to him waving about at the end of his stick-thin arms.

'No. Thank you. Don't bother bringing anything else. Please.'

He does not call for water when his mouth becomes dry, his tongue sticks to the roof of his mouth and he can barely swallow. He thinks of his sister, missing her. His chin trembles, his eyes leak precious fluid. 'I'm sorry,' he whispers.

Ashes to Gold

Jo Skinner

Lawrence found him. For that, Sara was grateful. With restrictions in place, no one came to the funeral—another blessing. She didn't want to face others' sympathy, pity, whispered condolences. At home, they placed Vincent on the sill in the attic where he once sat with legs bent to his chest, a book balanced on his knees, the steel vertebrae of the city outlined against the changing light of the horizon behind him.

When the urn fell, spilling ashes and ceramic fragments across the garden, it felt like a second death, Vincent's erasure complete.

Sara dissolved in a deep, black ocean of grief, resented Lawrence's silent retreat, his wordless acceptance of the way days bled one into another, sunrise to sunset, as if everything was unchanged.

Two months after the funeral was Vincent's nineteenth birthday. It took every scrap of courage to haul the weight of her grief up the narrow stairs. The door resisted her efforts before it opened with a sigh, and she found herself in the subdued attic light, her eye drawn to the empty sill, no longer able to separate grief, anger and guilt, the tumult of emotions raw, eviscerating.

Standing in his room again, it seemed he had stepped outside temporarily, would be home any minute, that the last god-awful weeks had not really happened. The austerity of the space struck her. The bed too small for his lanky frame, the blankets rumpled. His two pairs of jeans, the black stovepipe and denim hanging off the clothes horse, the jacket he always wore draped over the chair. With a small cry she picked it up, his scent faint in the weave, him not inside it.

A year before, Vincent started giving possessions away, announced one day he was leaving university. She longed to understand the depth of his disillusionment, arranged specialists, counsellors, terrified of his increasing melancholy, the way he gradually emptied himself until there was nothing left. It pushed the three of them apart, fractured their close-knit family. Sara taut with fear, Lawrence withdrawn, Vincent unreachable.

A tentative knock.

Sara startled, nearly called out Vincent's name, his absence not yet a reality. It was Lawrence, holding a cardboard box in front of him like he was offering bread and wine at the altar to be blessed.

Sara clenched her jaw, not ready to relinquish any part of her pain.

He eased onto the bed. It creaked.

She flinched.

He reached into crinkly tissue

Sara's fingers bit into her palm as she watched him pull out the urn, broken yet whole. Seams of gold like capillaries stretched across the surface, the lip uneven, a piece missing, just like Sara's heart.

Lawrence held it aloft, imperfections glowing in the light. Despite herself, Sara reached and traced the jagged path of a gold thread, until she reached Lawrence's liver-spotted hand. Trembling, she covered it with her own.

'Happy birthday,' she whispered, imagining the possibilities of being broken yet whole.

No Headstone

Em Readman

I find   the ring you gave me while packing up my rental. Nestled in a small, felted ring box, I notice one of the three pin-prick stones is missing. It is a gold ring, shaped like a wreath of olive leaves. I haven't worn it for a long time. There are still pieces of you lingering in my possessions; the ring, your signature on my early birthday cards, a few family portraits that hang on the fridge with a magnet over your face.

I wonder   what you tell people, what happened to your daughter? To say *she's no longer with me* is true. To say *she's passed on* is a mistruth. Often, I think about what you let yourself believe. I think about whether you think of me with anger or regret. I think about your new partner, if you've even told her you have children. I am long gone, but there is no headstone for you to mourn over.

I search   through my memories of you, landing softly on the better ones. I conjure up images of beaches and Sunnyboy ice blocks. Even in the aftermath, I find myself going back on my promise to never think of you kindly. I grieve these kind moments, knowing what followed. I grieve my half-baked daughterhood, thinking of red wine stains down your singlet, shaking at the sound of your voice. I grieve the time I wasted on trying to heal you, a child trying to put a man back together.

I ache   on September fourth. Friends flock online to praise their fathers, living or dead, and host barbecues in their honour. The emptiness you feel on this day is something you made for the both of us. Someone catches me in my head, staring at a card stand in a newsagency. *It's a tough day for me,* I say, and they pat my shoulder before moving on, almost knowing what I mean, never asking. I post a picture of my mother instead.

I soften   my shoulders, unclench my jaw, stop biting down on my lip. The man is not you, the one a few feet away on the bitumen. It could have been. You live in this town, not under it, not in the past tense I often refer to you in. You return from my memory in every man that looks like you, a spectre with greying hair. My body remembers you before I do, it forgets long after I have.

I bury   your ring, and your birthday cards, and your pictures in a box. I write 'Open When Ready' in permanent marker, seal the box with tape. I place it in my car and cover it with other boxes. You do not know the address that I am leaving, and you will not know the one that follows. I am moving to a place where you've never been. In doing so, I put myself to rest, and let myself recover.

The Gift

Carolyn Eldridge-Alfonzetti

In limbo
suspended
above my son's cot
waits a kite never waltzed by wind—
made for a boy too young to run
by a man too young to die

I picture my father's fingers
stitching cotton skin taut
over twine-bound balsa bones
yet knowing he'd not see
his grandchild's upturned face
and hear his joyful peals

In time
I will take
the kite, my son, and my sorrow
back to my childhood village green
and should the elements oblige
we will launch this symbol of love
high into an azure sky

to soar and dive as our lives

above a boy too young to remember
a man who longed to live

Passionfruit

Kylie Bates

You loved eating passionfruit. On Sundays I would return from the farmers' market with two packs of these misshapen purple balls, full of crunchy nourishment.

Your sister and brother would eat theirs with thoughtful consideration, mixed into yoghurt or spooned over ice cream. But you embraced your middle child instincts and devoured them as their name suggested. Standing over the kitchen bench—a quick, sweet satisfaction. You never put the empty shells into the bin that was right next to you. Always too distracted to finish any task. My motherly admonishments about your mess were never effective; you could spot the insincerity of my threats to stop buying them.

Sometimes I'd buy an extra pack, hide it away for later in the week. But I could never trick you, my cheeky girl. I'd enter the kitchen in the early morning to the evidence that you'd once again struggled to stay asleep. Restless, you'd searched out the hidden fruit. The morning bench stained purple, the scattered empty shells of your night-time snacking. Always insatiable, passionately searching for happiness in fleeting places.

So, I bought two passionfruit vines and planted them in our garden. I knew that it would take a few years of careful nurturing for them to grow strong enough to bear enough fruit to keep you satisfied. But I was playing the long game. I know that sometimes you have to be patient. I was planning for your future.

But you lived in the moment. Full of passionate impulsivity, unable to trust in a vague future reliant on the slow passing of time. Last season our vines gave us some delicious fruit, but not quite enough.

Now, I have an abundance of sweet, homegrown passionfruit. I hear them dropping with a muted thud onto our oh-so-quiet grass.

I have grown enough to feed my three children. But there are no more scattered empty shells on the kitchen bench. No more purple stains. A third of my passionfruit goes uneaten.

I hear you in those soft thuds.

The Cull

David Campbell

The sun cracks the earth like an eggshell and burns the air in a shimmer of flame. In the dry creek bed, ancient red gums raise shattered arms to the sky. It is early morning, yet already the heat is a physical presence that threatens the hammer blow of high noon.

I work the pump handle, and water, dirt-brown, gushes into the trough. Eagerly, the cattle bend their heads to drink. I hand feed, angrily kicking clumps of hay into the dust behind the ute. And my mind slips sideways to yesterday, the overpowering stench of burning flesh still heavy in the air.

I'd had no choice but to cull what remained of the herd. Too many beasts were starving and emaciated, skin stretched taut over brittle bone as they huddled in fitful shade. The waterhole, one last symbol of the river that had once blessed our land, was a sea of dark mud. And a graveyard for those that had gone before. So I dug yet one more pit and loaded the shotgun. My father had refused to do it this time. 'I can't,' he said. Over and over again. 'I can't!' And I saw the look in his eyes, the one that was always there of late when he was forced to put down a dying animal. The smoke cast a shadow against the setting sun, and he turned away at the sight.

Now he sits on the veranda and rocks in silence, staring blankly across the dead land. His hands, clasped as in prayer, flutter like broken-winged birds. My mother hovers, reaches out hesitantly to touch, but draws back, afraid, once more defeated by the flickering mirage of forty years that have come to nothing. He cannot hear her voice or sense her touch, and she has nothing left to give but tears. She weeps for him.

And once again my thoughts drift. To dark clouds gathering on the distant range, a mighty army on the march hurling jagged shards of light at the barren earth. To the drumbeat of rain on iron like the stampede of a thousand beasts, a sound that had terrified me as a child. To lifting my face to the tempest, with a vision of red gums in serried ranks bowing to a crystal river as it tumbles to the sea.

Instead I see a wasteland scarred with fence posts hung from sagging wire, like rotten teeth in a withered mouth. My father sits and stares at nothing, perhaps praying for miracles that will not come. For a future that is lost.

The bank manager coughs and shuffles papers. He watches my father intently. In a moment of absolute despair, I recognise the look in his eyes.

The Bally Wind

Louise Martin-Chew

26 May 2022

It is a year today. My father slipped away at 5:02—always the early bird—after twenty hours of unconsciousness. Today, the breeze is biting. The rain of recent months has cleared, with blue skies and fluffy clouds cartwheeling above my head. On a day like this he would have appeared in ancient corduroy trousers and the acrylic 'flannie' that comprised his winter wardrobe, slippers containing painfully swollen feet, struggling against *the bally wind!*

He was ninety: the first to say, *it's time.* He fell out of bed during a storm. With complications, the result of a 'long lie', he told the doctors there'd be no further treatment. I'd never heard it before, but a 'long lie' is a marker of physical weakness, illness and social isolation. Being unable to get up when you fall, spending a prolonged period on the ground, is so destructive to the body.

Suddenly on a palliative path, his only remaining ambition was to see the kids—and then go. He wasn't emotional, but found it quite exciting to be wept over as my daughter, Lian, left the next morning. Tallis, my eldest, came at lunchtime, her sobs hanging heavy in the wide hospital hallway. And Jasper, quiet, observed: after watching Grandma linger, Grandad is not keen to linger himself.

We became the property of the palliative care team, who listened attentively to Dad's wishes. We settled in, my brother, sister and I, morning and night at the hospital, the three of us in sync, fitting together in the same way as we did in a too-small back seat as kids. In this arrested, finite time, we talked and remembered our family adventures: childhood moves to Sydney, Melbourne and the Northern Territory; camping and off-roading in a Holden Belmont, broken trailers, buffaloes outside our tent, swimming in those brown rivers now crocodile infested. Those weekends as children were spent finding unknown places, exploring new territories.

Linda told me that, when I was out of the room one day, Dad said sleepily, 'You three are really brilliant. Especially because I am not really your father.'

It wasn't true. He married Mum with the three of us as a package, the only father we remember.

Those last days are crystallised, grainy in their texture. Even though I knew to expect it, when we arrived to find him unresponsive, I felt winded. It was hard to breathe, to acknowledge that my father had embarked for territory he had to explore alone. His body became cold, waxen, the atmosphere torpid.

We spread his ashes under a sprawling Banksia behind the dunes at his favourite beach, its branches a broad cocoon. There he's sheltered, the tree's canopy akin to the frame he created around the natural world for us. I remember his legs ascending steep cliffs before me, his arm supporting me in the surf, his gentle presence constant as we learnt how to be in the world. Now we travel on alone. The air is stilled.

The Taste of Bread

Mark Konik

It was the first time that I was glad my Baba was dead. I sat on the couch with a cup of tea that I let sit there and get cold. Foreign Correspondent was playing, and they were talking to a woman from a remote village in the Donetsk region. Like my Baba, she was hunched over and wore a scarf around her head. She had deep wrinkles and a peasant's features. The woman was crying at the thought of dying in wartime Ukraine. Baba would have seen her reflection in the woman. The rough hands from toil and a deep love of her country.

Baba watched the news dutifully each night. She would recite goings-on around the world. An earthquake in India, the American elections. But the news now would have had such an effect of grief and mourning on her, as the tanks marked with a 'Z' started rolling through eastern Ukraine and from Belarus towards the capital. Journalists reporting as the bombs started falling close to her family homeland of western Ukraine. A child running with her parent's phone number scrawled onto her back. Baba would have been heartbroken watching it unfold on her TV. I can picture her in her lounge room. She would have taken off her glasses, dropped her head to her chest and recited Hail Marys until the words got muddled. She would be thinking that maybe the more that she prayed, the more the war would go away.

I went to the Ukrainian Church soon after the invasion. I sat three pews back from where Baba had sat. I listened to the Priest recite the Liturgy in a mixture of Ukrainian and English. At the end of the service, he read a social media post from a family caught in Kharkiv. He stopped and stuttered at the line, 'We did not know the taste of bread until we had none left.' It reminded me of Baba pausing before she cut into each new loaf of bread. Like this man, she too had truly known the taste of bread in her life and now this hunger was returning to her homeland.

Now I think of Baba as countries argue over gas pipelines and whether a tennis players should be able to play at Wimbledon. I think of Baba and the villager from the Donetsk. The grief-stricken faces of the refugees and the soldiers moving to the front. I think of Baba and hear her voice say proudly, Слава Україні! (Glory to Ukraine!).

After Fourteen Years,
The Boorabbin Fire Finally Claims You

Renee Schipp

For Barry

Only now the woodland heals
fourteen years and still the mallee
cannot shed their stark dark sculptures
driving east on this same highway
                              the wide plain
imbibes, recasts its blackened
history in an inventory of blooms
bright bouquets made strange
by sadness

smoke bush, embers of grevillea
          held high in a late spring sky
subterranean, lignotubers
know nothing of hysteria
media, only how to know the light
absorb their loss, begin again

today we bury you in red earth
that always held you
in that patina, dust makes
all the graves seem soft, silent
the gathered crowd drops
eucalypt, scatter
of life over loss
sure scent of leaves
still unable to believe our love
was not enough to save you.

'On the 28 December 2007, a fire began on the north side of Great Eastern Highway, 80 km west of Coolgardie... [in] extreme fire weather conditions. The fire spread rapidly in a northerly direction in the Boorabbin National Park. On 30 December 2007, a strong northerly wind change caused breakaways from the containment lines... roadblocks were established; however....three truck drivers perished after [the incident controller] made a decision to reopen the highway.'
- Australian Institute of Disaster Resilience
https://knowledge.aidr.org.au/resources/bushfire-boorabbin-national-park/
and https://www.abc.net.au/news/2009-10-16/incident-controller-under-pres-sure-to-open-road/1106502

Mother

Jodiann Ball

I will love you when
your autumn tones tornado
into wispy winter highlights
when your knuckles knot
and your fingers fumble
and your lunch dribbles down your chin

I will love you when
your skin paperbarks and puckers and
your mind slips behind the clouds
and when I hold your hand and you say to me

Good Morning Nurse
My tube of rubbing ointment is empty
Please ring my daughter
She never comes to visit me

The Likeness of Sammy

KT Major

I'm trying to draw a picture of my brother, but I can't. Should be simple enough. Look in the mirror, draw my own face. But it doesn't look like Sammy at all.

The eyes are wrong, not quite lively enough. Maybe the lips should be turned upwards in that sometimes cruel, sometimes devastating smile. Or perhaps I'm trying to capture what Sammy's laugh sounded like: explosive, gleeful, ethereal, like a rush of cold air on a hot face. Will Mum remember, or is she trying to forget that too?

In the avalanche of goodwill, thoughts, and prayers after the accident, Mum took only one piece of advice: get a fresh start. For her, and her remaining son.

'We're moving on.' I doodle in my sketch pad as she resolutely packs the remnants of our previous life in cardboard boxes, eager to start anew in another town, caught up in the temporary solace that can be found in change.

No need for Sammy's clothes, which I refuse to wear. Or his ukulele, its strings silent and dusty. Mum shoves that in another box, with some notion of selling it someday. Next are the photographs, but it hurts to physically hold the sticky vinyl-covered albums containing the last known likeness of Sammy, perfectly preserved at age fifteen. So she puts them away quickly and methodically, closing the lids, sealing, burying.

Mum keeps mostly a straight face as she packs. But I know it's more wishful thinking than real fortitude. Rheumy eyes betray her, giveaway fissures in a patchwork facade that promises to crumble eventually. Not from a slight blow, but from internal ruination.

That careful veil of strength and order, even though she breaks a little when she looks at me. Or when she hugs me and wishes for two pairs of arms wrapped around her centre. So much like Sammy, but not him. Not her favourite.

When Mum isn't looking, I pry open the box and steal one of Sammy's photos, a celluloid facsimile of his smile, and put it in my shirt pocket, close to my chest so I can feel him. Other sensations come rushing, memories known and felt in my bones from a time before the day we were born: his scent, his breathing, his heartbeat as he curls up next to me.

But she soon discovers the open box, its contents violated. In rage, she screams and stomps around, looking for more packing tape. I watch her sadly. 'You can't keep Sammy in a box, Mum.'

No damn tape to be found, and she collapses sobbing on the bed, shoulders and chest crumpling inward, like her body is huddling closer around her heart. Mum begs me to forgive her, and we fall asleep, clutching each other, until it's time for her to go to work. Then the veil comes back down, and when I awake, the box with Sammy is sealed again and Mum is gone.

Last Song
Robin Loftus

I go to bed at night and hope to sleep,
wake to the morning's gaze and weep.
The sea no longer speaks in tongues I understand,
the sky, an upturned broken bowl
is emptied of its jewelled light.
The sun, the moon, the stars have left and I, bereft,
stare into blackest night without reprieve;
no song of birds, no rustle of leaves
to sweeten the darkening air.
You are not there my love.　　　You are not there.

Who Else Might You Have Been?

Michelle Brock

You are a man of few words, a breadwinner who disappears
at dawn and returns in time for tea; a man with calloused hands
whose paint-stained overalls catch the wind

and come alive and dance on the washing line.

You are a man who lays footsteps across the paddock in morning dew
while you teach your children how to tell mushrooms from toadstools.

A man who disappears to the vegetable garden nursing seedlings bundled
in moist newspaper and tied with string; a man who sweetens the soil
with cow manure before dropping seeds into the furrows you've made
by running your sturdy thumb across the ground.

You are a man, with rain in your hair, who comes inside smelling of damp
earth, or paint thinners after a hard day's work, or stale beer
if you drop by the pub on a Friday night and your wife's in a mood
because tea is ruined so you become a man who buys fish and chips
and a bag of butterscotch for your kids to suck while they watch TV.

When you retire you're a man who spends your days on handyman tasks
while your wife dreams up lists of home improvements.

On Thursday afternoons and Sunday mornings you slip off to the local
bowling club to win trophies that your wife despises because they take
you away from her.

Sometimes you long for a moment's peace. Sometimes you wish she'd just
let you be until you become a man who sits in the sun, hour upon hour,
listening to the radio and missing her, a man who tumbles memories over
and over in the silence of your bed.

You become a man who wakes up each morning on the frayed edges
of life and struggles to imagine who else you might have been.

For all my life you have been my father
and although I will never truly know you
these are the pieces you have given me to keep.

Figurines
Jennifer Harrison

You are dismantling her apartment
disinterring a china cup
from its chipped saucer
laying out the diamond tie pin

next to the German figurines
of a husband and wife threshing
the season's golden wheat
and another of a duchess

in a pink lattice lace gown
her tiny white thumb missing–
you undo the dress buttons
and climb into her exquisiteness

you disappear into porcelain
and find a small finger
among pearls in a herringbone wooden box
her wedding ring

no longer missing
the basket of roses spilling one last flower
to the carpet before you vacuum up
the dust left under the leadlight dresser

the cocktail sideboard
made from a captain's cabin wood
and then you pack the brass Three Wise Monkeys
in bubble wrap

and look once more around the room
seeing Xavier Herbert emerge from *Capricornia*
pen between undamaged fingers
Nevil Shute drinking a last beer by the shore

On the Beach
lying open on a bamboo table
while dancers glide silently into the walls
and you close the door to the sky

Two Birds, One Nest

Katrina Kittle

She blurted out tumbled-up names and nouns, my war-bride mother, battling her stroke-stumped speech. She kept tissue box tops, shopping dockets and mint lolly wrappers to tell me her shopping list. She hid unpaid bills in the pantry to fade and flatten under the '50s-green lino shelves, waiting for me.

She patted paw-paw cream on her lower legs—gashed and gulfed by ulcers—willing them to heal. Her beige bandages peeked through the side-slits of her maxi-length flower-print kaftan. She didn't flap about the surgery to sever and stump-stitch her legs. When she woke, morphine-drenched, she lifted her stumps like puffy fingerless hands waving a piss-off to pain. She learnt to slip on prosthetic legs, my gutsy mother, to stand steady with two sticks and walk straight.

She'd steer her wheelchair through our kitchen, then stretch up and over and into the kitchen sink, cleaning my dishes. She'd secretly wash some of her laundry, when it worried her, sometimes popping it into the oven to dry. She'd plonk three teaspoons of sugar into her cup, pour apple juice onto her cereal, and sip pharmacy-bought codeine cough syrup like it was lolly water.

She drove her chair into our home elevator and head off to bingo. When a taxi driver rushed and slammed her wheelchair into the kerbside, propelling her to the ground, slamming her buttocks from wheelchair to concrete, she sat silent like a wave-slapped seagull too stunned to flap. I stood silent, my hands clawing our veranda handrail, willing the driver to squat down and lift her.

She could easily slide from wheelchair to her shower chair, until her rotator cuffs run out of puff. Her occupational therapist was right: she must leave the house for rehabilitation; she may not come back. I could not look into her brown, deep eyes. She wouldn't want to leave. Her eyes wanted to stay sharply focused on me—the new mother—and the new baby. She doted, loved, doted. Two strong women in one nest, a psychologist declared, when I sobbed about my creeping estrangement with my mother, and of my dangerous, selfish thoughts. I felt suffocated and tired, a new mother making difficult, desperate decisions for her mother. My tired, old-hand mother was too speech-stumped to flap. She drove her chair into our home elevator, thinking she'd be fixed and coming home soon. Our mother roles flipped. I floundered.

She stooped into death's sleep with a shudder, my tenacious mother, in her late-night hospital room. I sighed and it did not feel right. I lifted a soggy tissue, like a wartime-mother farewelling her child-soldier. One of my brothers came, her youngest son, but he was far too late. For ten years my mother's secret things slept in her chest of drawers, in our home, waiting for me.

Birthday Girl

Sean West

for Aunty Sarah

              Your deflating balloons   skate
the ceiling,   their ribbons tangle you
in tentacles.   This is only your fourth,
the first of many   he's going   to miss
over decades.   You close   your eyes,
blow out your candles,   picture
the same wish   you'll make every year.
                          Your candles multiply
but the wish withers   like a sliver
of baitfish   in his palm
when he showed you   how he brings
home dinner after   long trips at sea.
Then he'd pretend   to swallow
the baitfish   and it vanished.
                          Your mum faces
the blade away   from her body
      to avoid   losing anything.
It comes up stinking   of chum
and oil slick.   The knife scrapes
the bottom,   so the birthday girl
has to kiss   the closest boy
                  but you shake your head.
You'll never wish   for a first kiss
      but to find the man   who dissolved
                  when you were too young
                      to cut your own cake.

Kite

Susanne Kennedy

You tug the string
that joins your arm
and the sky
inhales it back, feeling
how many ways there are
to dance.

It's a game of test and yield,
so like human-puppy play, only set
in a child's picture of sky: a wash
of smalt, albino fleece folded
through with a pinch of ash
thinking *how many ways*
there are to see.

There are just two points
to this quivering square,
its equal reach
to heaven and here.
The intermittent stall—mid-air,
behind ribs—that has you
fill the air with murmuring
spitfires; giant, tissued combs
rippled by, surely deliberate, sky breaths.

Until it's no time
before you're lost
with upturned face
in a smooth-awkward waltz
with mischief and longing, in this way
of holding while letting go.

Water, Salt and Gingerbread

Lauren Ward

My fathers' house still smells like my mother. It is a specific mix of her favourite Dior perfume, and a gingerbread candle she would light every day to make the kitchen smell as if she was baking something delicious. Typical of my mother, to trick us into thinking she was making anything from scratch.

At first, I thought the smell would disappear over time. It's been ten years now—ten years of dad cooking chilli and of my brother spilling beer, of sawdust tramped through the hallway and covering the bathrooms in bleach—but it is still here. I think perhaps Dad wants the scent of her around.

The cats still know the sound of her voice. Their little fluffy ears perk up. They turn and stare like you have said something offensive. Maybe we have. They don't like to be reminded of their abandonment, and neither, I suppose, do we. We have painted over the colours she chose for the walls and replaced the trinkets that sit on the mantlepiece, to try to give some semblance that this house has moved on.

For a year, Dad was impossible to reach. He rotated his reactions to his depression, but the result was the same. One night, he sobbed until he had no water or salt left in his body. Another night, he went on a walk that lasted five hours, my brother and I watching out the window, anxious for his return. He talks of never coming back, but he always does. He takes us to the cinema, and cries through his popcorn.

It's better now, I think. We still miss her, but it's in the smaller, harder to explain ways. We miss her on Christmas morning, when my father turns on the radio for the first and only time of the year, to dance quietly on his own. We miss her when the first rose of the summer blooms and there is nobody there to demand that it be displayed whilst we eat strawberries and cream in the garden. My brother and I missed her when we begged to be allowed to go to a festival, when we got our first tattoos and Dad ignored us for a week, when it was prom night and she wasn't there to fix the button on my dress.

Mostly, though, we miss her when we go to see her and her new husband. She doesn't feel like Mother now. I am not sixteen anymore, and

I can see that she is happy, that she thrives and is living the life she always dreamed of. I can even be happy for her, in a distant and half-hearted way.

The truth still sits there though, hidden in our pretence that we have grown out of the grief. This loss and sorrow that we feel over losing her is never one that she will share with us.

Homecoming

Shey Marque

*'Once upon a morning I woke up being a bomb
and flew headlong home'* — *Lesyk Panasiuk*

I wake again, eyes like pilot lights. My mother is still asleep in
the next room, but I'm not in the same house where I lived as a
child, & this does not feel like home. The bed does not feel like
my bed. When I roll over, my hips find hollows left by cycles
of children, & the only thing that sleeps is my arm. I'm here
because of the bomb wedged in her cerebral cortex. It's just
light & I can hear sustained whimpering.

She's curled
up on the carpet, wedged between bed, table & wardrobe. I
have never tried to lift an adult off the floor before, the full
weight of her carried on my thighs & calves, my labouring
breath. A tiny assassin sits on my palm—round, white, waiting.
Picture it navigating its way inside vessels, the stealth of it
crossing over the blood-brain barrier, lining up its target, the
rupture. Part of me breaks off, guttering & spent. I leave her to
sleep away the chemical morning.

In the kitchen I am
burning myself on microwaved oatmeal & banana. Exactly
why I am coating my tongue with sugar & press it to the roof
of my mouth, I can't recall. I'm hopping through walls,
tunnelling-time barely discernible. In one room she's small &
I'm checking for bruises hiding in her hair. In another, it's me
who is small, ripping the head from a doll named Grindl, *home*
going off inside my hippocampus.

Death Watch

Jenifer Hetherington

my father's chambers are of ancient oak—
reverberate with the syncopated ticks, cuckoos,
chimes of three clocks—

strident Westminster quarters mark his flown hours.

something is gnawing,
we sit to wait through the dark of the night,
tap tap, hidden deep, tap tapping

ancient timbers creak, groan, crumble.

beetle larvae chew faster,
adult males tap tapping, calling a mate
to come tup tupping

my father lived an opera drenched with death and desire.

his Swiss watch runs a day, a month, a year behind
howls that his timepieces, his children
all tell him lies

sad tales hang as dry leaves on a dying tree.

obdurate time slips and slides through the night,
silence is raucous, tick, tap, tick, tap,
out of sync, out of joint

stop the cuckoo, still the pendulum, yet there is tapping.

it's the wind, knock knocking, tap tapping
a different key—a storm at the end of this longest of nights—
a sapling taps the window, day comes in.

My Grief is a Mandala

Rebecca Ryall

Although it is spring, the day is cold. A steady drizzle dampens everything, despite the marquee I have erected. We are accustomed to being here when the campground is full to capacity, with families enjoying the spring break from school. At those times, we wandered the park, dropping in on friends for a game of cards, a round of bocce or glass of wine. It seemed the entire population of our small town demobbed and regrouped here and we existed in the easy embrace of friends.

This weekend, though, the campground is quiet. Our little mob clusters around the large fig, five or six campsites set up with only the rudimentary requirements—we are here for a weekend after all, not the usual two weeks. We are seven families, bonded by friendship and tragedy.

We laze around the campfire cooking food and drinking cups of coffee, trying to ignore the not-quite-rain, rugged up in ugg boots and jackets. As the day draws on and the weather worsens, I anxiously await the turning of the tide. I've misjudged the times and feel the cohesion of our group slipping. Tired of waiting, I take my daughters down to the beach. We walk as far along the small bay as we can before being blocked by the tide and the tumble of fallen paperbarks on the shore. Along the way we collect shells, seaweed, feathers and pebbles.

I carry a basket of rose petals.

We are silent, contemplative, as we construct the mandala. With a piece of tent rope tied to a stick, I inscribe a circle, then segments and embellishments, which we decorate with the treasures we collected from the beach. I walk the circle and sprinkle the rose petals, crouching low lest they fly away in the wind.

It is cold. Suitably cold.

As we work, I watch our friends descending from the headland, beginning their slow procession down the beach, heads bowed as they scan the ground before them, also collecting bits and pieces along the way. One by one they arrive and in silence join us in our sacred work.

I take from my basket the horrible plastic urn and wrestle with the lid. Slowly I walk the outer edge of the circle, scattering the remains of my eldest child around the mandala. I offer the urn to each of my daughters in turn and when they are done they pass it on to friends. We all take part in this ritual of sending her back to earth in this, one of her favourite places of all.

When we are done, we make a circle of our bodies, hands clasped, enclosing her in our embrace one last time.

And then we turn and walk away.

Annabel

Catherine Edwards

It starts with a stutter a falter in the natural order of
        light that chases
shadows and I say your name over and over like a prayer
        my heart knows

your marshmallowy soft hands
        clasp and release
lungs stammer and stretch in your tiny chest as you thrash
        and fold

remaking yourself into something new and how do I close the gap widening
        between you
and me lasso time your toes like tiny snails curl as you try to
        grip hold to

hang on this world spins and tilts and I fall from my
        axis to be
in this endless millisecond between the worlds and my DNA
        unfixes and rearranges

itself into something unknown and unstable and your eyes open and you
        breathe a breath

        that lingers in my bones.

Echoes of My Mother

Yvonne Patterson

is there anything else
    you want to know?

last night I tidied echoes of my mother
    combed through fading photos
        the farm girl, war years, fiancé's death—

today I sit, wait, stitch her name
    in nighties, cardigans, a dressing gown, fold her
        inside a room, too small to hold her

she tidies memories, I listen—
    is there anything else you want to know?

        —our worlds recalibrate
lifetimes ricochet between

her bed, my chair, my hand
    and hers, my eyes and hers, her lips
        my mouth and hers—her voice

so frail now—confounds my wish to ask
    to start back at the start, reboot, or
        just complete the gaps—if I ask

will she summon strength
    fight morphine mists, retrace
        the space between — if I ask

will I keep her here
keep her here
keep her?

The 10 Main Elements of the Universe

Jenny Pollak

When I woke you were lodged between the 5th and the 6th vertebrae
of my spine.

You whispered through the gap

between my stiff ribs the physiotherapist said
he couldn't get the width of

one finger between. The flesh where the heart has not quite
sealed itself off.

I haven't dreamt of you for a long time.
I think hunger is like the tide.

In my dream
I led your signature away from what was required

to be your legal guardian.

Love made it necessary to chaperone the truth.

Hydrogen
Helium
Oxygen
Carbon

ash from one of them at least.

Your name dissolves into hands scrolling
the page like two birds. We're both falling

as we laugh,
as the horizon drops its guard and returns

to the distance
where we are both held.

Neon
Nitrogen
Magnesium
Silicon

Iron
Sulfur

Today it is different.

Today the sky is titanium with grief.

You won't be admitted

until I allow that flesh be abandoned.
Admit that everything was borrowed.

July Night

Jo Gardiner

The house in Katoomba is dark and silent
when I arrive. My friend is here.
Birdlike. Old. Alone.
Two cats and two terriers watch
us eat curry together. She pours me a glass
of red and sets it down carefully in front of me.
A minute later, she leans over the table,
snatches up my glass and drains it in one gulp.
I wonder about the way things don't work out
but remain unsolved; death declines resolution,
doesn't comply—is oppositional in nature.
And you don't know that until you've watched
how it behaves a few times.
I don't offer platitudes.
She plays the cold-voiced message
from the friend who said don't come—
the exclusion of that worries at her like a sore
that refuses to heal. How ugly our human hearts
can be. There was no letter or message for her
at the end. The loss falls hard on her.
Outside, wind gusts stalk the night sky
and peel all clouds away
to leave the moon pale and stunned and stark—
an upturned face receives the bad news.
As I leave, the concrete birdbath
by the photinia hedge looms
like a gravestone
crouched there in the dark.

The Graves

Damen O'Brien

Something of yourself goes into the grave.
40 years since you last saw them, save
an email at Christmas, your father's news
of cousins' weddings, family barbecues
you never attended and the inevitable run
of deaths and funerals, that generation moving on.
The last time, you were really young
and the white-haired brigade wore hats and sung
Nearer My God to Thee and the women
wore flowery dresses and flowery perfume and then
they tossed a scoop of soil upon the bones
while you and your cousin ran among the stones.
Into the grave, the last person to recall
the way you were when you were small,
the bagpipes at your uncle's beery wake
while you hid under the trestles, scoffing cake.
Into the grave, your uncomprehending grief
the day they laid that little box beneath
the silent soil, only eight months after
the baby showers and the laughter.
One by one a part of you is tossed
in amongst the wreaths and dirt and lost
and you'll be eating sushi in a bar,
a country and decades away from what you were
and you'll be caught with something in your throat
and try to wash away that sour note,
the moment when you read that she has gone
into the grave, her funeral long done
and you'll be the last to remember after
you place your mother's rings beside your father
into the grave your memories are bound
and then you too will one day go into the ground.

Super Hero
Lisa Barron

I felt myself sinking to the bottom of the pool as defeat washed over me—a strange feeling. A dark face appeared and swam to pull me up. He was a super hero flying under the water to rescue me. He carried me to the side of the pool. I don't remember how he did it.

He became my greatest friend. He was the second Aboriginal person I had met. I was eight.

The first Aboriginal boy appeared with my mother's distant friend. We only spent a short amount of time together but it was magic. We walked through the bush next to our house. He wasn't very talkative and seemed sad but we enjoyed each other's company. He left and neither he nor his mother returned to visit.

This second boy was happy. He had the biggest smile. He could swim and run, and he loved to talk. I could barely walk and he was asthmatic. That's how we came to live together for a short while. We were both at the John Williams Memorial Hospital for Children—a hospital that rehabilitated children with disabilities from polio. I didn't have polio. I went there to learn how to walk again with remodelled legs. I was born deformed but walked anyway. I needed them to be remodelled so I could keep walking into adulthood.

I don't remember his name…I just remember fun.

On Sundays we went to church. I had to go in my wheelchair and he used to push it and race down the hill. For the first time I felt like I was running—the sound of his laughter, the wind against my skin. This was freedom.

The hospital had rambling gardens big enough to get lost in. That's what we did one day. It was my first walking adventure. We set out over the little garden wall and just kept following a path until we could see the main road. My super hero showed me flowers that we could eat. They were crispy like chips and tasted tangy.

No, I don't remember his name. I just remember fun and his smile.

I left the hospital and his smile left too, as did my happy memories. He wanted to come home with me, but the matron gently told him that he couldn't, despite all my enthusiasm to make his question a reality. We wandered off sadly. The adults talked. It was crushing to say goodbye.

Mum and dad talked about him in the car. They said he had something called foster parents who had taken him to the hospital but wouldn't take him home. They talked about how the matron took him to her home whenever she had days off. My eight year old brain struggled to understand why anyone would not want a hero to be their son. I wondered if they even knew.

The Last Supper

Ian Stewart

I have to do it, but it is so hard to bear, spooning the hospital mush into his mouth. He looks at me with each spoonful, a look of incomprehension, child-like in its wide-eyed uncertainty.

The stroke has cancelled movement down one side. His speech is all but absent. Drool dribbles uncontrolled out of one side of his mouth. From time to time there comes the occasional release of flatus. Once, solid stuff emerged, accompanied by an overpowering odour. I turned away then, gagging. It was all I could do to stay the distance. But I have to. He is my father.

A towering figure of my childhood—always happy, smoothing my worries and tending to my cuts and bruises. I can remember him ladling ice cream into my waiting three-year-old mouth. And there were other things, less attractive. But I never rejected a spoonful, no matter what it was. I knew he wouldn't give me anything that wasn't good for me. 'Good girl!' was his constant remark.

Then, those golden days at the beach, zinc on the nose, holding his hand—almost out of reach—as we strode to the surf's frothy edge. Always a reassuring, safe smile. Mum would come too, holding the other hand. Hard to remember her. Taken from us by an errant motorbike at the shops one Saturday. I was six then.

Now he's reduced to this. Not much more than a vegetable. If I close my eyes as each mouthful goes in I can—just for the moment—envisage us at the zoo, laughing at the monkeys, awed by the elephants; unwrapping bright Christmas-papered presents together. And, when I had my own children, there he was, spooning early solids in, mouthful after mouthful. 'Good boy. Good girl.'

Will there be no end to this terrible decline into sub-humanity? The doctors say that another stroke will carry him off. Should I wish for it, pray for it? As I wrestle with this thought I put another spoonful in. More dribbles out onto the bib.

Two nurses arrive. 'If you don't mind, we'll wash him now. We'll be about ten minutes.'

I rise, weary from the effort and drained by the emotion of memory and of the reality that is my father now.

Outside, the air is fresh. The hospital garden is arrayed with roses in bloom. There is life all around me. Ten minutes and I'm reinvigorated. I turn and go back in.

At the door of his room I stop. *How much longer can I go through this daily grind, providing my beloved father with the nourishment he needs so much but can hardly retain? But I must do it.*

I push open the door. He's there, sitting upright against his pillows. Shaved, hair brushed, all neat and tidy. Is that a smile on his face? His eyes are shut. I pick up his hand. The wrist is limp. His head lolls and his breathless mouth sags open.

It Isn't Like That

Lucy Nelson

You tug. I'm only flirting with sadness. It isn't serious. Not yet. I cast long and suggestive looks its way: my mother's small address book, her neat handwriting, the packets and packets and packets of medicine whose flimsy cardboard has outlasted her body. And we swap glances like this in hopes of connecting, despite feeling nothing at all.

There are moments when we almost touch — sadness and I — but they are only accidental. I take my parents' bin out to the kerb. On the way back up the driveway, this house and this car appear suddenly to belong to one person: her husband, my father. My sleep is still trained to stay in the shallows in case she calls out in the night, because her absence is not a fact again until the morning. Just like a body losing strength to stand alone is not a fact until the moment it must be lifted from the edge of a bed. These vaporous new truths multiply and harden.

I wonder if guilt is the way into sadness. I hold in my mind phone calls it took me a week to return, conversations I cut short, boredoms and frustrations I did nothing to conceal. But sadness knows that game too well and retreats as crudely as it was summoned.

Instead, it draws my attention to a green plastic chopping board, whitened with knife-scars and dust from the pills we cut into pieces and pressed into babyish lumps of fruit purée for her to swallow. Within four days of her dying, I replace it with a shiny wooden one. Its clean, un-storied surface is a detour that sends sadness back the way it came. I play hard to get. I make moves that threaten severance and erasure.

Eventually, I suspect sadness is dancing with someone else. I take a hint. I let go the idea that it will appear. Perhaps we are incompatible. I begin to think I have only imagined the thread suspended between us. For a nauseating moment I sense it is simply cut, but then my mother — or some newly lost piece of her — pulls it taut from an invisible end point, from wherever it is she and sadness have been dancing together. And with no thought of life or death, no taste for games or for glancing, I feel my way blindly along the slimy stuff this rope is made from. I hold the points of weakness in hands her body made.

Our First Christmas Without You

Karen Lowry

I am watching the Christmas lights flicker
like my holiday spirit. Our tree is plastic
and covered in glass ornaments.
Over the fireplace,
stockings, tape that holds up the garland.

There is duct-tape on the roof also.
Really, we are all just taped together;
we are presents left under the tree too long, the tape
no longer sticky;
life does not stick to us the way it did
when you were here.

Here I am watering plants that outlived you.
This hot summer, dry like your skin in those
last few days. Shallow cheeks like
a collapsed souffle.

Here I am in the kitchen singing Christmas carols,
baiting the holiday season with bird calls,
leaving cookies and warm milk on the bench.
We follow footprints into the new year and wonder
if we should give up hunting, sell the guns,
buy game frozen from the store, instead.

Lasting Impressions

Carmel Macdonald-Grahame

Of Music—   When rain drowned the house on the riverbed,
it remained a mess until insurance was settled.
In the silver lining, her flute survived the flood.
We rehearse here in the afternoons, she said.
We finish on time, but best not arrive too soon.
So I did, and heard her spin music out of air.

*Of Housework—*I take real pleasure, she confided to me, in cleaning.
I subside into it and wiping, sweeping rhythms
set my thoughts adrift. I find such labour sensory,
an immersion in dream, a mental respite, uplift,
and order, of course, is ever its own reward.
Poetry, in comparison, is hard, hard work.

Of Bell-Ringing—   Oh she could ring the changes, in syllables
timed to a pounding heart, could feel the tingle
in her fingertips of bell-chamber silences
giving way to the aural thrill of peal and knell,
knew the ropes, hauled long old-world tethers
into towering notes, bringing them to life.

Of Teaching— Just write, she said. Villanelle, sonnet, sestina…just….
Oh, just think of form as poetic technology and write.
Release yourself into the form and *then* invent. Just
Do not waste time waiting for poetry to arrive,
Inspiration is the least of it; just write. You'll see.
Even an acrostic might deliver what you least expect.

Of Poets—   Regretfully this poet must decline the invitations
showering her decades like confetti. Launch books?
Judge? No, never. Competition? Slam? Lord forbid!
Poetry is a far cry from all that, she would insist.
But other poets, otherwise compelled—praise them!—
did what needs-must, to have her art take flight.

Of Words—   In a note of thanks for it, she confessed that in years
of cloud-watching she had not heard the word, *Virga.*
This phenomenon of rain failing to reach the ground
and creating grey halfway-curtains of ragged cloud
is a sublime image, we agreed, and signifies, surely,
something more than weather—a grieving sky, tears.

Come With Us

Bill Bean

In the morning, the crows called across the valley.

They were not usually there. Somewhere else must have exiled them and they hunched their blackness in the trees like cast out priests. Their calls were an echoing loneliness.

The dawn came slowly, diffusing the dark like milk into coffee, clouds layered with pink, the light pushing sleep away. The bed was warm and the sounds of others in the house calling to one another echoed the crows; parallel existences.

He knew he wasn't abandoned. Someone would come in a while. They were just getting on with their lives. Sooner or later someone would come.

Three years passed since the accident and optimism had dissolved into resignation. His world had shrunk to a view from a bedroom window. Once, he had been carelessly vigorous, paying little attention to mobility or health and the accident was like a lash, slashing with malice and determination, unheeding of consequence.

The tractor cage saved his life and he wished now it hadn't. His back was broken and it hurt. All the time it hurt. Hurt beyond pills and reassurances and not just his body but his psyche. To be dressed and washed and carried was an ignominy after a life of doing. The family mourned with him but their mobile lives excluded him. Not intentionally but they had to get on with it and he lived on the fringe of their physicality.

So he waited, and soon the coffee came and the wheelchair and the clothes and the push to another place in the house for the day to stretch out and out until another night and another dawn.

He read a lot, travel books, and remembered. Bush and mountains and streams running. Cattle in the back paddock in grass high to their knees. And he cried remembering.

They put him into the SUV with the necessary baggage and they went to the sea, to a headland with the sound of waves below and the wind strong from the northeast. They set him aside on the grass while they got the picnic out.

Beyond the cliffs, swifts flew against the sky and as he watched they dispersed, disappeared and then reappeared tumbling upwards in wild abandon on the updraft, spearing into the sky like tossed balls, repeating again and again. Not feeding, just living, tumbling, turning, calling. Alive.

Their exuberance carried him with them and separated in the moment from pain and pessimism, joy came again in just being and the feel of the wind on his face was like the earth's breath.

And, when his family came to gather him in, he smiled.

Sugar Snaps

David Terelinck

I picked the sugar snaps today,
pulled each plump pod from the vine.
I remember you planting the seeds;
your need to turn sod, feel your hands
mittened in loam. The puckered furrows
made me think of your suture line
where the surgeon gingerly weeded
in order to sow you more time.

I picked the sugar snaps today.
The knuckled pods so like your fingers
spindled by disease and time.
The slugs beat me to the turnips,
parsnips, and kale. I don't mind, really.
There were too many for my use
and I'm just not up to swapping
condolences for excess veggies.

I picked the sugar snaps today.
Not because the weatherman said
the first frost was on the way.
The bite of an early winter
has already blanched the colour
from my days. I picked them
because too much around here
has gone to seed already.

Tomorrow, I will prune the roses.
The garden was always your
domain; I remain all thumbs,
none of them green. But I'll learn
to start the mower, reason how
to spray for scale and aphids,
gauge how much is needed to fill
each lingering hour and season.

Wounds

Jason Beale

In old Japan
the Jizo stand,
forlornly waiting
for life to return,
stone to be reborn.

For many years
I was an outcast
from this land of
broken love and
a miscarried child—

silver-scaled and
smeared in green,
the koi slipped
through my dreams
like knives.

Wounds so strange
never really heal,
and sometimes
silence is the
kindest measure.

Golden-eyed and
living in the light,
my children now
are love's return—
forgiven and fulfilled.

You Always Said Black Isn't a Colour

Jane Frank

The world we shared is a painted surface. I design a toposcope
of places and days —

remember the way we used a palette knife to load up unmixed
joy in colour?

Now you're gone, I pour closely over all I can see, pare down
shapes — mountains, roofs, fields of cane

areas of positive and negative space — the parts that perhaps
needed more work,

measure the distances back to waterways of connection in
steady strokes —

heartbeats? before leaves tensed on branches and the clear
air started to shake

The final marker on the orientation table of us will say 'where
you are now'

I try to imagine a place (beyond the horizon or exactly where
I sit now) where raw umber and magenta pool,

where a hillside is lined with a crisp silhouette of eucalypts
in late winter sun, the sky never darkening

Pandemic, a Villanelle in Time of

Tric O'Heare

In Memoriam K.M. 19.10.1988—7.11.2018

You would have thrived. Forgive the irony,
but I just want to be honest with you
in this world alive to its mortality.

We all now breathe air thinned by uncertainty,
wide-eyed in the darkness familiar to you.
You would have thrived—forgive the irony.

There is a tilt in our society
that might have meant we got the keeping of you
in a kinder world alive to its mortality.

Clean hands, (don't laugh), acts of generosity,
moral integrity—an ideal world for you.
You would have thrived—forgive the irony.

But you turned away so resolutely
just over a year too early to be you
in this world alive to its mortality.

Dread. Hope. Unpredictability.
I don't know how else to say it to you.
You would have thrived—forgive the irony—
in this world alive to its mortality.

The First Morning

Ann Shenfield

I'm barely awake, I'm in my pyjamas
Perhaps I'm still asleep and have slept through everything

In a persistent dream with its insistent howl
and years later I won't know if I'm one of the bawlers

My sister is yelling *shut up shut up shut up stupid*
don't you understand anything?

But I don't understand, I stare at the window—so much light streams in
it might be biblical, I create and recreate the fall of light

That surrounds a shape on the floor
although much later—perhaps it's only today

I recognise there never was anything on the floor by the window
in the collective mania of the dying father

Light streams in the window as everyone colludes
I'm in my pyjamas playing my part

My mother howling, blubbering, ululating
and this incremental, inexplicable numbness—which probably also comes later

For now my mother flails, a trapped wild bear
who everyone says I need to protect

In the morning light my father slips
into the mirror before it's covered over

And I'm already a canary like the one that used
to fly around the kitchen

Whose cage was shifted to the alcove
Who would later escape to sky or the mouth of a cat

Perhaps I've flown into the mirror
with my father and have become a song of air

While he is made of words, which remain unspoken
then slide into silence—words that existed once

But now are only pockets of light, I glide over them, but catch on phrases
captive in the mirror, as the child who plays at me becomes proficient
                                                        in her role

The howling, growling mammal is anaesthetised
her wound cauterised, and my sister is already Sisyphus

I can see him he's with me, I tell her
She's a tiny, exasperated Sisyphus who'll do anything

To shut the idiot up, to not have to keep this ball rolling
to not let the mourning break

The Things I Miss

Sherry Mackay

'Can you do this button up for me?'

I turn to him and do up the top two buttons of his pink striped shirt. Later he asks if I can take the lid off the jar of pickles. I unscrew it and bang it down on the bench, an angry sigh escaping me. I feel angry, and so I feel guilty. We eat the dinner I have cooked, him holding a fork awkwardly with fingers bent in several directions. He cannot use a knife so I make meals that only need a fork or a spoon. He has clumsily carried his plate back to the kitchen, one edge resting on his forearm and the other gripped precariously in his fingers. I wince and pray that he doesn't drop it.

When we were young, we walked along holding hands. One day I asked him why he wasn't holding on properly.

'I am!' he protested. But he wasn't.

I loved riding pillion as he took his motorbike up into the hills, until one day he couldn't. His fingers could no longer grip the handlebars or change gears. Oh how I miss that bike.

Taking photographs and building things disappeared from his life too. He used to make things and build things and cook things. One by one, 'things' disappeared from his life, from my life, from our lives. I mourned them, god, I mourned them.

And children disappeared too. Well, there were none—yet. But there never would be. I often thought about how clever they would have been: his smarts and design flair, and my orderly, librarian brain. How I miss those never-born children.

I yell at him, more often than I should. And I feel guilty and mean. And angry. Let's not forget angry. I grew up with a father crippled by polio, and a mother who was undoubtedly angry too. I always swore that I would never be her, so when I found him I knew I had 'done good'. He was tall and fit, clever and capable. I vowed I would never be as sad and angry as my mother. Clever me. Stupid me. But the gods had other plans. Hubris, just stupid hubris on my part.

I loved how he would do little dances for me, shaking his booty, twerking, jiving. These days, he cannot even hug me while standing up.

He has no balance, and his legs shake. I miss hug. I miss being swept up in his arms. I miss that capable and clever man. And so I am now the handywoman of the house. I learn how to drill and screw and putty and paint. I climb ladders and fix things. I reach up dangerously higher than my head to move things, and repair things.

And I am angry. The anger makes me mean; the anger makes me sad. The anger is really fear. I miss that young husband. I miss our old life. I miss me.

Footprints
Lyndal Weightman

It's spring, and you run ahead of me on the sand. Laughing, you turn, your hair flicking across your joyful face. 'Leave nothing but your footprints on the beach!' you shout, as you gather a piece of paper fluttering in the breeze. Looking back at our footprints, we smile, and from that day we call that stretch of coast, Footprint Beach.

Summer comes, and still you jog along the beach, turning to look behind, glancing at the soft sand fringed by lacy foam. 'We should leave nothing but footprints wherever we go.' You pick up an old plastic bottle. Your right leg falters and you limp as you reach the bin.

In autumn when we visit Footprint Beach you are walking. You try to jog but stumble. Still you manage to smile through your wisps of dark hair blowing in the wind. You tell me you've been to the doctor. And I'm sure you have been many times already, to appointments you pretend didn't happen. You give away your vintage china to family. Your tapestry is posted to an old friend.

It's winter and we walk slowly along the sand. Your breath is laboured. You shiver in the icy wind yet throw your arms out and say, 'Isn't it wonderful!' You clutch my arm for balance as you reach down and collect a discarded wrapper.

You bring a picture and fix it to my wall. It's your beautiful painting of Footprint Beach, the white sand patterned by multiple sets of footprints becoming smaller, shrinking to dots then disappearing. 'If only we could leave nothing behind on this earth but footprints,' you say as you labour over lifting the picture, straightening the painting.

It's spring again, and you give away what's left of your recycled furniture.

I push you in a wheelchair along the promenade by the beach.

'Stop!' you call. And stretch to pick up a piece of tin. You turn, 'No footprints to leave now, just tyre tracks.' You smile under your beanie, then say, 'I wish to be free of my possessions. I want to leave behind the smallest possible footprint on the environment.'

You give away your beloved old bike, still working after all the patching and fixing over twenty years. My heart breaks.

And then you are gone. It is too soon. It was always going to be too soon.

It is a long time before I visit Footprint Beach again. It's a beautiful spring day and the clear aqua water laps gently. I hold my daughter's little hand, watching her tiny footprints form behind her on the sand. She looks up at me through a curtain of dark hair, and smiles her grandmother's smile, your smile, as she picks up a piece of paper for the bin.

Your footprints run through my heart. I can't begin to count the things you've left behind; there is no measure for what remains of you in those still making footprints in the sand.

vale Jill

Christopher (Kit) Kelen

and thank you
for your words
they live
to catch our breath

things in the view
and the view
will be gone

but today we will meet in your book
that's a conversation
in a garden

where no words suffice for wonder
though they are all that we have

things in the view
and the view
will be gone

today it falls to us to flower
it is beautiful to have been

today we are reading your words

your words as alive
as last week
as next year

our hearts are lit their way

You Were Packing Boxes

Kathy Shortland-Jones

I sat on the floor next to the couch where you rested,
my head near your knees, close to the teapot,
so I could pour gingerly for you,
pass you small bites of brownie:
a treat from the kind pastry chef down the road
who knew you were dying.

We were surrounded by boxes of memorabilia
of musicals and sports days and swimming carnivals,
of classroom photos and bright posters and glass ornaments,
of earnest hand-written cards to you for changing spirits,
lifting bushels, shining lights.

You were packing the boxes because
you didn't want your husband to have to cope with them—
he would have to manage everything else:
the house, the cleaning, the cooking, the lunches, the shopping,
the comforting, the planning, the instruction manuals,
the warranties, the receipts, the emptiness, the cold linoleum,
the hollow bed, the love,
the grief, the boys.

When I asked you: *Are you scared?*
I sensed your answer before your mouth filled with terror
and I moved to the couch to cradle your body,
swollen with steroids and pinioned by an imploding ache to see
two young boys grow to become good men.
When I wanted to ask: *Do you believe in something?*
my words swallowed themselves and I wiped away your tears.

You were packing because
the boys would be everything
that he needed to focus on
when you died, leaving a space so magnificent,
so gut-wrenching, so gracious,
that he cannot possibly clear out the memories.

Everything I Had But Couldn't Keep

Claire Williams

It's another loss, I said. Like when Patrick died.
HOW DARE YOU he said HOW DARE YOU SAY THAT.
It is, I said (now that he didn't love me I was free to speak my mind).
I lost him and now I'm losing you.

In the car, after the phone call (something had happened)
racing to the hospital to see what it was, what horror crouched, waiting for us
(the terror, cold terror).
I said, *please God, please God* and he said, SHUT UP SHUT UP.

Afterwards, at home, friends gathered. And he drove back to work.

Next morning, lying dully in the empty bed, I heard the garbage truck.
They were still collecting the garbage.
Why would they still do that?

The counsellor was bereft.
It's terrible, he said, just terrible, slumped in the chair.
It's ok, I said. We will be ok.

For weeks, acquaintances would ask lightly,
"How's the baby?"
And I had to say.

We are not parents now, he said, so we have time, we can concentrate on our careers.
(I knew that was wrong. Quietly, to myself, I resolved I will not make the best of this. This is not OK.)

Insistent lyrics describe for me the loss
of my baby
of my love

I thought of you as everything I had but couldn't keep*

*Lyric extract from The Velvet Underground "Pale Blue Eyes"

Tea Minus Three Months

Shey Marque

We keep missing each other inside the house, as though existing in different moments kept separate by a severed particle of light. A collapsing point appears on the sofa where she opens her fist & liberates a hummingbird moth, raining scales from its wings as it hovers. She's listening to a voice in some other air. *You know she wore all my clothes without asking & I'd get so angry.* For the third time I ask how she'd like to mark her upcoming birthday. She pulls a face. *I haven't given it much thought*, like it isn't anything important, like it isn't going to be her last. Storm cloud on the back of her hand, she picks up both teacups, walks to the back door. It's so hot out there you can see heat waves. I say I don't want to sit outside. Her face tells me nothing but her hand offers up another moth, its caterpillar body wailing like a kettle. I'm thinking of the woman, her house full of cold tea, leaving cup after cup in every room &, not able to locate any one of them, spending all day returning to the kitchen to make more. By now, my mother is outside & the tea is lost for colour. I find her overwatering the hanging pots of bee balm & many clear-winged moths scatter. When we hug, she hinges unusually close, her sheer honey blouse unfurling & flapping against the easterly wind.

When a Man Cries at Dinner

Sharon Rockman

Sunday night. At Mopho on Carlisle, you sat across from me and cried.
I broke off my own tiered tirade; dropped my chopsticks to listen

as the restaurant receded and your tears dribbled and shone—
Harper dying on Wednesday night. You couldn't find him. But knew.

18 years old, ginger and beloved. You heard soft pitiful mewls—
Tracked him by the tile around his scrawny neck to underneath

the house, directly below your ensuite. So, you got the toolbox,
and by 2:30am had the carpet prised away and the floorboards

gauged. You flattened yourself to crawl belly-like through spaces
impenetrable, black and filthy to retrieve his stiff lifelessness

that you fitted into a box, feeling guilty about the curvature
that might be disrespectful—When I asked about the floor

and ruined bathroom (I saw pics), you assured me that you would
willingly have prised apart the house entire for that old cat,

which blurred and morphed into how you missed your mother
who passed away just months back after an epic stale stint in hospital,

which rendered you small, curved and confined. As it was you who
had to tell her she wasn't getting out. You who made those first arrangements

for her brittle translucent casing the night she passed in that bed,
on that ward, in that fluorescent room. You who sat alone on a bench

outside the hospital entrance at 10pm to call an old friend who didn't pick up—
It was You. Sitting across from me; the plastic table sticky with hoisin sauce.

Lest We Forget

Brenda Proudfoot

On the Fernleigh Track,
the whine of wheels is a warning
as a pack of curled cyclists
race by. We walk in harmony,
our lives untouched by war.

A dad, in an earbud world,
pushes a stroller: his infant son
slumbers, his nascent brain
lulled by the tok of swamp frogs
and the strum of the board walk.

We pause at a reedy pond,
scouting for egrets or spoonbills.
An armoured turtle surfaces,
he flicks his back flippers,
submerges in the tea-stained water.

A swarm of native bees forms
a halo around a tree hollow.
From his paperbark perch,
a butcher bird dives in a dogfight,
picking off bees like an ace.

We remember our fathers:
your father recorded battles
in his BBC voice—the needle
etching the wax platters stuttered
with the shock of exploding shells.

Mine, a wireless operator
flying over the Pacific, relayed
enemy sightings in his Morse
melody of dits and dahs. On
being a gunner, he was silent.

Our fathers were witnesses
to the cruelty of war. Here,
we tread lightly on an ancient
wetland as fragile as a world
teetering on the brink of war.

Spring in Albuquerque
Kerry Greer

The car accident happened at 20mph in a parking lot on campus.
The passenger side, where I sat, was struck, and I watched the other driver
through my window, her daydream cracking like a cicada's exoskeleton
as she realised what was happening, the breeze coming in through the windshield
all over her skin. We could have made eye contact it was so close, so slow.
Shock can roll down the body like this: leisurely kiss along the shore,
and wondering where it might end —the gentle line of white-
wash they call *the break.*

     You were driving me to a dance class before
the car accident, and I said: *It's ok, I can walk there. I still have time.*
You took me by my shoulders, and said up close: *Baby, you've been in an accident.*
You're not going to any dance class. Everything seemed like A Big American Deal
to me. Eventually I agreed to stay, to provide a police report on this very slow accident
and let my idea of the future float away for one evening. Later, we ate curry
at a Thai restaurant with a lopsided drive-through bay, faded image of a burrito
below the 'Lotus Palace' sign. I stared at the sheen-black countertop flecked
with grains of rice, pale fingerprints, wondering: Who really lost the plot?

The insurance company said our car—with a single dented door—was a write-off.
They paid for us to see an osteopath, and when she asked how my neck pain had started,
I told her it was the car accident. She leaned over her clipboard, ticked some boxes.
Then her fingers found the knots that were always there, always returned.
Not long after, you went away.
That last day, I was getting Raphael ready for the playground. Holding him, trying
to dress myself, strange fractals of panic in my throat, and a phone call that split

the seam of my life with its noise, white ringing in my ears. For weeks
I woke into the deserted bed—two thoughts only in my head:
You had gone to work early in our new car.
I would meet you later on your lunchbreak.
Then your face a ghost up close to mine in the grey bedroom, the breeze dusting
my shoulders from the open window, everything split wide—and something cold
that was not the air but my own skin, raw and not yet real—
But (*let me past you, I know where I'm going*)
if I could just lift Raphael over the crack, we might reach the playground still,
find you waiting outside your office on campus at lunchtime.
It's ok, we can walk there. We still have time.

Gran

Abby Partridge

My best writing tip is editing. Make changes. Ruin, recover, repeat.

Today, I don't want to edit. I want to sink into a beanbag, like a sugar into a frothy coffee. I want to watch *Fly Away Home* and stand with my back to an open fire, drinking lemonade from a green metallic cup, while my mind collects all the wrinkled memories arriving in snippets and waves. How is it that I've only lived this long but all the memories stretch out for a hundred years?

You don't know how to grieve until you're grieving. I couldn't have predicted that I would want to read poetry like a Hail Mary, over and over, trying to find somebody who has felt the same. Then again, maybe the right words don't exist until someone writes them down.

So here I sit, your youngest granddaughter, penning a strange and transitory letter to the co-author of so many of my earliest recollections.

Today, you were sleeping until you weren't. I bet your dreams were of your pony, whose name you never forgot, even when mine had disappeared. You didn't hurry. You just said, 'It's time I hung up the bridle,' and rode, dignified, into the Great Something.

When I got the call, I was transferring blackberries from a bucket into tupperware containers; my fingertips stained purple while I separated those that were still intact with those that would only be useful for filling a pie. A task that feels both wildly inadequate and beautifully fitting. I wonder how many blackberries you picked in your lifetime. I wonder if they came from the same brambles as these, next to the fence that Pop built, and along the creek where we swam as kids.

I already miss the farmhouse, where I would jump from one coloured lino square to the next and peer into the top of the piano to watch the innards move as my siblings mashed the keys. Where I would ride the red scooter down the hill over and over, on a slope that now seems much too gentle to have frightened me when I was six. You taught us reality (a shotgun for a snake); risk (fuel for a healthy fire); and reward (a ladder for the best cherries.) You were always there to catch, comfort, and care.

You can edit writing, but you can't edit life or death. While I'm here trying to find all the right words to say, put them in the perfect order; move the punctuation so that it sounds—just—right … I can hear your voice as if it was yesterday. I've collected all the eggs, and the car engine is already running, and I'm reluctantly abandoning the open fire's warmth, and the tv guide is under my arm, and I'm unlatching the front gate, and I'm stumbling on the concrete in my soccer boots. Your voice follows me as I slide into the back seat—

'Ta-ta—see you soon. I love all you kids.'

The Silence of Grief

Karen Young

Grief shadows me, silently walking beside me, reminding me of its presence. And reminding me of the grief of others. At the movies. On television. In books. In life.

Perhaps it's similar to when you buy a red car and you notice red cars everywhere.

The red cars have always been there.

The grief has always been there.

How did I not notice the immeasurable loss that constantly surrounds us?

I read somewhere that your grief is like your fingerprint, unique and personal to you, and I feel the lonely truth of this.

I miss you.

Not your soul or spirit, but you.

The you whose body birthed mine.

The human you I knew and loved.

It's irritating when people say you had a long life. Or that we were blessed because you didn't suffer with cancer for very long.

It was long enough to extinguish the preciousness of your life.

Is that not suffering?

I am eternally grateful no one has said to me, 'She's in a better place.' Hearing those words would definitely push me over the edge of restrained politeness.

People mean well. I remind myself that their grief too is unique and personal to them.

Grief keeps me connected to you, and oddly enough, I fear a time when that connection fades. When my world no longer feels broken without you in it.

Will that feel like a betrayal?

In other moments, I find myself completely lost, staring at your photo, willing you back to life.

The closest I get is seeing little pieces of grey hair scattered across the dressing table in my childhood bedroom. Neglected remnants of a home haircut. It's comforting to see them there when I visit Dad. They're the only things left on this planet that contain your DNA. Apart from my brother and me, of course.

I can't bear to move them. How could I ever suck them up into a vacuum cleaner as though they're worthless?

Whenever I stay with Dad, I dry my hair in my old bedroom and my heart lurches each time a few of my stray hairs float down and land silently on top of yours.

When Dad dies, someone may as well torch the house because it would break my spirit to wipe out the physical presence of you both with my own hands. Especially your precious little grey hairs.

Apart from me, who would ever understand the significance of those discarded hairs? Not a single soul.

To the outside world, life goes on and all of that, but on the inside, the grief-induced silence is deafening.

Sometimes the silence overwhelms me so much that I crave standing on a cliff top, screaming and screaming until there's no sound left inside me.

It astounds me that grief has no voice of its own. Surely it should be the loudest sound imaginable. A guttural screech that pierces the heart and reverberates through the soul.

Grief deserves to be heard.

Winter

Jo Gardiner

That July, Dat was reliving the death
of his twelve-year-old sister not long
after they arrived by boat from Vietnam
thirty years before.

                 Sometimes he'd text me
and we would walk along the Paris End
to the cliff above Moon Rock and sit
and talk. This time,

               it was just before
dusk. We sat side by side on the
rock, our voices low. It was clear to
the west; in the southeast, clouds lay
in soft lilac piles.

            We fell silent. A single
black cockatoo slowly waded through
the great expanse of our silence, threw
down a cry from time to time. It was
unusual to see a solitary bird—

                 usually,
they fly in mobs or pairs. As it
passed high above, it cocked its head
and looked down at us, then continued
on to the clouds.

            Its cries faded and dis-
appeared as did our bodies in the rolling
dark. Like water at night, our faces held
the only light. By the time we each turned
into our separate gates,

            it was completely dark
and even our faces had gone.

Seraphim's Last Song

Kate Maxwell

Miss Navarro won't let us crawl
under desks during maths
       she never says 'shit'
or lets spit stream down her chin
but now she's fallen over Michael
in the reading corner and both
are leaking red and still as stone.
        I'm leaking too: legs piss
sticky, wobbling like jelly
crouching level with two dirty
Nike sneakers stomping past
my shaking table: smell of pencil
sharpenings, farts, and something
like burnt rubber
          boom in my ears, blood
on my tongue, heart hurting
in my chest and scream stuck
in my throat while I wish for wings.

Gabriel's head is open like his eyes.
I squeeze mine shut so all I see
is Mom. She'll have to wash my pants
because I can't go to Little League
like this and we won't win
next week's final if Michael cannot
move cause he's our best striker.
        Raphael is weeping
way too loudly beside me.
Shut up. Shut up I hiss and think
of that thing Dad always says
when we're out buying bullets
        Guns don't kill people; people do.
But here's this gun busting open
bodies in my classroom
and now it's pointed straight at me.

Precious Cargo

Virginia Muzik

San Francisco airport, en route with you to Oregon. Gathering my carry-on luggage after the security X-ray, my mouth is dry, my skin clammy. I know they'll pull me aside.

A cobalt blue-shirted form approaches, a robotic male voice states, 'Ma'am, I need to ask you about a powdery substance we detected in one of your bags.'

His eyes fix me with the cautious stare of someone about to expose a felony. This scrutiny unsettles me further.

'Y-yes…i-it's some of my late brother's ashes,' I stammer, my voice croaky with nerves. My late brother's ashes. I register these words, but drift off from the woman I hear saying them. My eyes dart to my hands, watching them fumble in my handbag. 'I have the papers here…'

Those hands now awkwardly brandish an envelope with the death certificate and 'Disposal of Human Remains' form in front of the TSA officer. He waves my hands away, shaking his head.

'I'll need you to get the contents out of your bag,' he instructs.

I silently obey. With stilted moves, I retrieve the small cardboard gift box that contains the white fabric pouch that contains the plastic ziplock bag that contains your 'powdery substance'.

More like crumbs than powder, I'm reminded, squeezing your remains in my palm.

When I'd first touched what the flames had reduced you to, scooping you into this bag, I was surprised I felt no emotion.

I watch the TSA officer take the bag in his latex-gloved hand and walk behind a counter with a high screen that obscures my view.

Without warning, my world drops away, like it did when you died. A sudden weight crushes my heart, forces the breath from me. Panic jolts my nerves, like you're leaving me a second time, and I just want what's left of my brother back—NOW! I steady myself against this surge of separation with both hands on the table, planting feet beneath jelly legs firm on the floor, trying to still my trembling bottom lip, gasping in air.

My mind slips back to that time in our thirties on that Oregon beach, the one I hope to return you to. We're trudging along the sand, our bodies whipped, our eyes stung by the salty winter gusts, singing together – a moment in tune, in synch.

The refuge of this brief memory dissolves when the TSA officer returns. He hands me back the ziplock bag, with no, 'Thank you, ma'am', no, 'Sorry for your loss'.

Winded, wounded, I scramble to collect my belongings, eyes scanning for the nearest restroom. Once inside a cubicle, I slam-lock the door as my composure unravels. Bags fall, sobs heave from my core, my legs buckle and I collapse to the toilet seat before I can undo my jeans.

Rocking gently forward and back, I whisper, self-soothing, 'It's okay, I'm safe. You're with me now, it's okay,' checking and re-checking I have the bag of your chalky crumbs.

Of Birth and Death

Belinda Bishop

I want to crush my young self to my chest, looking back on the grandiosity of our hope. He left uni to stack shelves to rent our townhouse, begged for hand-me-downs, salvaged a high chair from council pick-up at twilight. In my chrysalis of pain, he drove me to hospital with P-plates earned weeks before.

In our first moments, my eyes wide and wild, she is so small, all fingertips, mauve-pink skin, and rubbery chord. Naked together in the white bath, incomprehensible thing accomplished, her skin is warm butter, just as my grandmother described. What words does a mother have to describe her firstborn newborn creation? Delicate point of cheekbone, elegant half-moon swoop beneath her eye. These will haunt my longing for years.

Cord cut, bath drained, moments drag as I find words. *She isn't moving.* The midwife, dismissive. *She's very still.* Midwife, rubber gloves. *Bit of oxygen.* And she's taken from my arms.

A bloodied tube, HIT THE YELLOW BUTTON, alarms and air electric as she vanishes. Frozen, I'm lifted from bed into clothes loose in the middle, carried recoiling down shiny harsh corridors, flailing in all my being but hypnotised in my body, to the threshold of her last place.

This cannot be said. There is a table. May your children never lay on this table.

A rectangular light, machinery, and, at the centre of the Earth, her. Newborn ribcage, ventilator, thin skin and curled bone. Butterfly flight peppers the mechanical pumps. She sighs, her own breath, her Elan Vitale. Spread and floppy, tubes snake from her mouth, crisscrossed wires, plasters of cats and teddy bears. I am weightless lead.

Gently avoiding tubes, my mum strokes her skin. I am paralysed, so she holds my hand and I stroke with my thumb. Perfect brushstroke eyebrows cinch. *Tell me she is not in pain, liar.*

Under the doctor's pen light, her silver irises are stunningly beautiful, but motionless against the sweeping beam. Feeding tubes and nappies stretch to the horizon, her perfect brain disintegrates like froth. I can't stand, a chair slips beneath me.

In our arms, her breaths quiver. I am undone. Blood flows from her nose, and horror and love stretch me wider than I knew possible. Nine months, three hours, and four minutes. The sun has not risen on her first day.

Carried by family through the predawn, we learn about our daughter and the signature of death. We sway and stroke and murmur, committing details to memory. Her fingernails, ten miniscule seashells of deepening purple. Plump body, not curling but opening like the palm of a hand. Soft skin, cooling and wrinkling, pricked blue with the adrenaline that kept her with us until the end.

The end. Earth pivots, spins in reverse, and the story folds back upon itself.

Leave hospital with empty arms, as we came. Take down furniture put up. Belly wanes barren and flat. High chair secreted back to council pick-up under night.

Neighbours do not ask about our baby, so very, very loved.

Dear Mum
Jo Rendle-Short

Dear Mum

Last week, all six of us (your children, now adults, all still alive) had a slide night on zoom. Finding each other (again) during lockdown. Tiny postage stamps across four time zones. Remember those Saturday nights when we'd hang up the white sheet against the back wall, put the carefully-chosen slides into two long cassette boxes (turning them back-to-front and up-side-down), wait in anticipation for dark to fall? Remember the fun, the laughter, the ooohs and aaahs?

One of the slides (suddenly, without warning) was a large photo of you and me. There we were, sitting on the front steps of the Sheffield house. My child-hand on your knee. Your mother-hand around my back. Pulling me in, holding me close. Your face awash with love.

'She loved you most, you know', came the sibling claim, swelling into a heart-wrenching stillness. *No, I didn't know,* I said silently to myself, thinking, *what happened to that early love? How did its silky softness slip away to reveal the harsh coldness of a jagged rock?*

Last night, my brother and I wondered (aloud, questioning) how you could have said the things you did. We were genuinely perplexed. Was it your belief in a rigid and righteous God? Your determination to live a spiritual life? We jointly reminisced, gently lifting delicate strands of memory. Searching for moments of touch, for warmth, for attention and love.

We spoke of you. You, who left us with scars, with memories of hurt. You, who clouded our minds with confusion (still). You, who hated the way we lived, the way we brought up our children. You, who insisted on conditional love.

This afternoon, I watched Sarah (my wife, who you haven't met, who you would probably refuse to meet if you were still alive) cut her mother's finger nails. There's an intensity, a tight concentration. *That's love,* I say to myself. Bodies close, chairs touching, heads bent. Eyes emitting kind concern. Quiet talk allaying confused fears.

Each day, Sarah asks for her mum to be brought down to the front door (Covid rules). We look on as her wobbly body emerges from within the cocooned nursing-home space. Wispy white hair, hands outstretched to distant walker, noisy shuffle of dragging feet. We watch as she turns the corner, peers through the glass sliding door, waves at our silhouettes. Before grinning widely. 'You're here,' she squeals with joy, yesterday's visit already a misplaced memory. I look on as Sarah throws both arms around her, kissing her cheek, holding her close (while desperately trying to keep Covid safe). Faces awash with love.

Daily, I'm witness to this mother-daughter, daughter-mother, love. I observe its attentiveness, wonder at its airy lightness. I cry out (silently) for our love (yours and mine). *Where did it go? How did it slip from our grasp?*

Daily, I'm reminded of you. Daily, I imagine a different story, a love-filled story.

Thinking of you,
Jay (third daughter)

107

Autumn Shades

Anne Casey

A chill south easterly is buffeting the last
of the rhododendrons, lodging their
gaudy protest against autumn's steady progress,

stirring memories of other rhododendrons far away
among the winding lanes of Mount Callan,
boughs meeting overhead, to dissect
the sky into glinting shards, a glitter of lake
reflecting here and there between the lush profusion
of blooms—violet, cerise, lilac, cloud-white—walking
side-by-side with my father, the shadow of grief still circling,

his hollowed eyes, deflated cheeks, his tentative feet
barely touching earth along this grass-grown road
he had strolled so many summers arm-in-arm
with my mother, clutching you then in his great
powerless hands, your fine platinum strands drifting
on lake-breath to tickle his bristly cheek, and—
as if you knew—you threw your head back, electric-blue
eyes crackling a silent current between you, your small fists
hinging, lit face wide-open to take in all those wondrous
new colours, a lone red gumboot marooned
somewhere on the trail behind.

I never cut fresh flowers from our garden
although almost year-round, I could take my pick—
camellias, clivia, hibiscus, gardenias, lily-white monstera
cones, the delicate pink bells of the *Elaeocarpus Prima Donna*
ragdoll-dancing on the breeze, jacaranda lilac-carpeting the path,
Magnolia Grandiflora and frangipani perfuming the air—
their names as lovely as their sudden unfurlings.
I like to watch them linger, fade on branch
or stem, alongside the newly budding.

Maybe after school I will show you our late-bursting
rhododendrons, tell you how once—before you
can remember—you salved your grandfather,
taught him how to carry his living
together with his dead.

Closure

Kathryn Bennett

It's an ordinary day—a Saturday, and breakfast with the newspaper, my weekly treat. The magazine is my favourite section, and I turn to the Quiz. I'm hopeless, but I continue our tradition since she left. Today I scored only five, though I learned that an isogram is a word with no repeating letters.

On the opposite page the Kitchen Sink Drama* usually gives me a wry smile with its minimal word count and unexpected twist. Today my eyes are drawn not to its title but to the capitalised words on the third line. 'CALL ME. URGENT'. Despite my inner voice raising caution I read it, and now I'm back there.

It was another ordinary day—perhaps rather more than ordinary as my gardening muscles were receiving a TLC massage. 'Call me. Urgent'. Not a text as in the magazine piece, but a voice message from her husband that unravelled my tranquillity when I turned my phone back on. It was the moment my world changed.

That was several years ago, and yet, this morning, my gut has taken the same punch it received back then. My mind is a cocktail of that day's events, her funeral, my life ever since, and the devastation encapsulated in those four syllables.

Today I find myself focussing on that banal question that members of the press always trot out at times of tragedy. On the steps of the courthouse after the sentencing of the culprit driver I'm asked if this means closure.

How could I know back then that my deepest wound would never be closed? That on any ordinary day, like today, something could spear into it with pinpoint accuracy and excruciating pain? Sometimes it's the sound of an ambulance siren. It's being asked who is my next-of-kin. The other day it was a car advert on TV. And every year it's Mother's Day. Today it was having breakfast at home with the newspaper, reading a whimsical short story about how a girl missed her mother's call and consequently a bargain purchase. Each time it's different and takes me by surprise. Each time it's the same spear that pierces and re-opens my wound.

Closure: it's an isogram with no repeating letters.

Closure: it's a concept for no repeating traumas.

Closure: it's an expectation of others that can never be fulfilled.

*Paul Connolly, GoodWeekend, Sydney Morning Herald, March 26, 2022

Home Stretch

Carmel Macdonald-Grahame

Our father is close to the horizon, his biology has been scanned
and handed on a silver disc to his children, who see right through him.
He gives it gaunt attention, man-in-the-moon, eyes filling
with radioactive information—the oracle, after all, foretelling
his last heartbeat in a language he can't speak, but written in light,
so he believes it. These are now his facts of life:
he is entering weeks that will be subdivided by hours and minutes
spent shedding weight, as if intent on zero, or his only appetite
is for lifting-off lightly at the end.

Days are accounted for needle by needle, pill by pill
swallowed in daily acts of will with the news of his own subtraction.
We, filial, shoulder the chemistry of nourishment, the arithmetic
of protein, iron, carbohydrates, cell hydration, his survival
a calculation of withering proportions, as he, protean,
shrinks his way down scales that seem calibrated for disappearance.
Until he is dividing time between sleep and sleep, durations
growing as night and day lose meaning, and as if he had decided
to spend hour after hour until his last minute, practising.

Siblings once more, we face off across birth order, revising old hierarchies
first, next, last, son, daughter; contesting trivia, from family recipes
to who put whom in charge of grammar, giving way to the legacy
of our mother's blessing, by sharing the labour of medication,
sustenance, hygiene, trading rest for the vigilance of careful conversation,
wheelchair journeying to keep the roses pruned, filling vases for his
fragile pleasure.

Sharing the intricacies and intimacies of the last parent's death
we know we are witnessing the vivid brevity of a generation,
breathing-in the reality of life's speed, as it catches up to us.

His days reduce to the number of steps from bedroom to kitchen;
or expand, so the distance between bed and chair fills existence.
Affection works hard while he clings to his skeleton and we try
to be undaunted by unsettled silences, unanswerable questions,
capricious outbursts, cantankerous nostalgia about long-ago offences.
We are learning forgiveness, that it is never too hard-earned;
paternal flaws barely flicker in childhoods measured by the absence,
his and ours, as this departure closes-in promising no arrivals, no returns,
and, already grieving, we wait with him.

Edie

Danny Kinnear

At first you didn't seem real but then we heard your heart beating so fast and strong and saw the funny little bean on the ultrasound and the presence of you—this new person in our lives started to sink in. Then Liss could feel your kicks—so faint to begin with but growing stronger and stronger until I too could feel them under my hand. What an incredible, world-shattering, exhilarating feeling! So much power and energy in such a little form. I would talk to you and be answered in kicks and flutters.

The weeks passed quickly and then in the darkness of the ultrasound room we received terrible news. You had a severe genetic condition. We scoured the internet and found stories of people who had overcome the odds and also stories of intense suffering and hardship. It was heart wrenching and we cried with so much anguish and devastation imagining your future. After a week of talking with specialists we decided that it wasn't fair for us to bring you into this world with so much possible pain and uncertainty waiting around each corner.

We then found out you were a girl and we named you Edith Rose. We took you to our favourite places, ate our favourite foods and took you to hear the voices of your family. We asked our loved ones to write letters to you and we read those out loud so you could hear their love on the morning we went to the hospital to say goodbye. In the darkened room the procedure happened quickly and suddenly you were gone and Liss and I clung to each other as our grief poured out of us.

The following labour was long and Liss so incredibly brave. When you finally came out, so tiny and so beautiful and were passed up to Liss all of the midwives were crying too. At the funeral home we laid you to rest on a bed of leaves and flowers Liss had grown, along with roses from your grandmothers and great-grandmother.

After you were cremated, we thought about how the carbon that was in you would be absorbed by a tree or a blade of grass and how your water molecules were now in the clouds and would fall as rain to sprout seeds and grow plants and journey to the sea. In a small ceremony we spread your ashes under the ancient oak here and our close friends and family hung flowers in its branches to honour you.

Early the following morning I climbed the hill on the farm and watched the sunrise and I felt an intense sadness that I wouldn't be able to show you all of this wonder and beauty. Then as the golden morning light spilled across the landscape, I could see you in the forest and in the pasture and hear you in the magpie's song and knew that you were all around me—intricately part of the universe.

To the Woman Playing Candy Crush in the ICU Waiting Room

Lisa Kenway

if you dread going back in there
dream each time you visit him
of sunburnt skin and greasy fish-and-chip
fingers
licked clean, of beach runs
hand in hand and race you to the flags
not parched lips blotted with paraffin
tube tie's angry welts
the whale-song ventilator
a limp one-sided grip

if you wish you spoke
of advanced care directives and finances
knew what he wanted
when you could still ask
how to change a tyre, mow the lawn
cremation versus burial
machines and doctors or home and morphia
the ocean laid out before you

if you listened when he told you
you can't win a battle without hope
belief is our biggest weapon
in this fight to the death
if you sit and wait and nod
and sign forms
hardly noticing the horizon,
forgive yourself
you're here now
and in the end
it's all
that will matter

Drive

Geoff Forrester

Never put off for tomorrow
what you'll never have to do.
Don't worry Dad, don't sweat
the conversation we'll never have to have
and I won't sorrow either
for that gift of tongues
we never developed suddenly on a drive
through the Southern Highlands.

And nor will I lament our lack
of a heart avalanche, brought on
by terrestrial triggers of hedge and lush farm
and expansive green paddock,
a fertility giving permission
to some raw confession of filial piety
and, quid pro quo, a reckless response
of shocking parental tenderness
mugging us both
with love through thickets
only fifty years in the coming
but now ripening rashly,
blindsiding us both with a sudden fruition
into naked declaration
and a showing of hands,
side by side and eyes ahead
in the tight little tin
of this humming Corolla cab.

No, I reckon it'd ruin for us both, Dad
such a rioting in our cells,
such an unfolding of legs
and brushing of spiders from a long put away
card table in the shed.

So let's have a quiet pie at Robertson instead.

115

Goulash

Kathryn Goldie

It is the smell that does it. I am at the front of the shop, peering into the darkness, not sure it's open, when it hits me and I step backwards. I am about to spin back out, onto the grey footpath and into the chatter of voices and the hum of engines, but a small, wiry man emerges from the kitchen.

'Yes, we are open,' he says, with a slight accent I recognise.

I manage a murmur. The aroma has engulfed me and taken my words.

He looks at me. One eyebrow lifts slightly.

I want to tell him that I am somewhere else, two decades ago—or is it three?—sitting on a chair in my grandmother's kitchen, safely away from the stove, watching her cook. Her hands are small but sure, with deep creases and lines, and she rolls the dough—so much of it—into little green-flecked balls, golden in the sun.

'I want one!' I say, legs swinging on the chair, and she turns to me, smiling.

'It's no good till it's cooked,' she says, her accent swirling around the room and tickling my ears.

I frown.

She laughs and brings me a dumpling. In my hand it is damp and cold and no longer gold. I poke it once, twice, three times, till it falls apart, a floured mess with bits of chives. I look up at her.

'Taste it,' she says. A strand of white hair glows, backlit in the sun.

I shake my head.

'Roll it up for the pot, then.' She gestures with her hands, a smooth deft turning. I am clumsy, and try to squash the dumpling back together.

She takes my hands and guides them gently, and seconds later a dumpling appears on my palm.

'A little water will fix,' she says, retrieving it. And soon the dumpling is back on the tray with the others, moist and golden and waiting.

I watch while she chops the meat, the tomatoes, the onions, the herbs. Flavours it all with salt, pepper, the red smoky spice I can't yet name but will grow to love. She measures by eye and by taste. The scales someone well-meaning once bought her stand high on a shelf she cannot reach. Grease and dust gather on them.

She hums a tune, sings in a language I don't understand. The kitchen grows warmer. There are bubbles in the pot. She slides the dumplings in, and they dance in the bubbles. She turns the orange-blue flames down, and we wait.

The man touches my arm, and I jump. 'Are you alright?'

I nod, shake my head. I think so, I don't know. I am at my grandmother's table feasting on goulash with chive dumplings. But the table is gone and the kitchen is gone and so is my grandmother, and the Hungarian restaurant on Bondi Road can never bring her back.

Wet Kitchen Bench
Mitch Browne

I wipe the kitchen bench
and it sheens with mother
of pearl from the overhead
halogens.

The slick crumbless surface
mirrors the one
Grinkov and Gordeeva glid
over on my black and white
tv in the children's ward.

Gordeeva said she knew
Grinkov would always be
there to catch her but later,
when I was stronger and
he had left her for a heart
attack, she cried in colour
at my house.

My own marriage flared
equal and freestyle and all
was paired performance
but now, the division
of labour has slipped
into separate routines:
she creates and I clean up.

The bench is clean and wet
and I see them iridescent
in their prime and on the ice
around them are two halos
from our kitchen lights. There
should be three, but one blunk
out, and I haven't replaced it.

I know she doesn't like it
when I leave the kitchen
bench wet. But it will dry
soon enough without any
help from me.

Field of Mars

Ian Wicks

On looking up, at sixty,
there were flashes of lightning,
even with my eyes closed.
At the hospital, a young doctor
examined both eyes carefully,
then pronounced it was not uncommon
in myopes of my age –
a posterior vitreous detachment.
As though a storm was brewing behind one eye.

I flew back to the harbour city
and a colonial cemetery,
named after a god of war.
We are here to bury the ashes
of our gentle, widow mother
and our rebel sister – that headstrong girl,
her precious thunder and lightning
surrendered too soon—
in our father's grave,
in the Field of Mars.
I have not been here in over fifty years
because I could not vanquish
a trailing sadness,
and that name, the Field of Mars,
has haunted my lexicon of grief.

Ageing eyes still flood with tears
and I am once again that child, bereft,
come to bury family
along with Sydney's invisible dead
in this careworn ground,
beneath the vast translucent sky
adrift overhead.

A Moment Shared

Kylie Gardiner

We sit facing each other, each in white hospital gowns. I'm twisting my ring around my finger and she's rubbing the gold chain around her neck. Anxiety rips through my body. Her eyes are closed and her chest moves rapidly as her breath comes and goes. Then she opens her eyes and sits on her hands. We acknowledge each other with the faintest of smiles. Neither of us has a phone to fiddle with. It's just each other.

I want to know why she's here but I don't want to push or offend. Finally, she speaks and I'm grateful.

'Are you here to see an obstetrician?' she asks.

'Yes,' I answer.

'Me too.' I can't stop shaking.

'I'm a ball of nerves.'

'I'm losing my baby.'

We immediately move from strangers to confidantes with one revelation. Then out it tumbles, our past pain, our uncertain futures. We are both waiting for confirmation that our pregnancies are viable. 'Viable'. Clinical. Sharp. A business transaction. Something workable, feasible, practical. Not the gentle, sweet language of a baby.

We discover we both have three-year old girls. We talk about how our losses have made us so grateful for them. I tell her our first pregnancy was a premature stillbirth which wrenched us into a club where things can go horribly wrong. And here we are again.

She has had four miscarriages since her daughter was born, some as late as fourteen weeks — the stage we are both at now. Her current pregnancy has been fraught with bleeding. She has come straight from her corporate job where she feared she would lose this baby in the sterility of the staff toilet. We agree that if our current pregnancies don't survive, we won't go around again. Too much loss has crippled us.

Then a nurse comes to take me through to the ultrasound. We each say 'good luck'. My husband is waiting for me. Standing stiffly by the door. I lie down and the obstetrician smooths cold gel on my abdomen. Then she brings the monitor forward. She watches it carefully while pressing the ultrasound across my belly. We tense.

The screen flickers and pulses. It is not long before the obstetrician switches off the screen and closes her hand over mine. I've had this conversation before.

'I'm sorry,' she says.

This second opinion is the same as the first. 'Not viable.'

Numb, we stand at the reception desk. Then we see my new friend leaving. She turns to us and places her hand on her belly, then gives me a thumbs up. Her face full of relief. Then she looks at me with an 'and you?' question. Her eyes alive with expectation. I pause. I wait a second. Then I give her the double thumbs up. She smiles broadly and waves as she goes. Amidst loss there is still joy.

Leila

Lesh Karan

In the gloaming, you always appear
as an eight-year-old with ebony-brown

hair, like mine. I can see you twirl
and cartwheel across a field of tulips

because that'd be y(our) favourite
flower. Lightning bugs hover

in the fore: I will them to frame you,
so, I can see an illumined vision –

do you have my freckles on your nose?
Your dad's molasses skin, his tongue

in my cheek? My logophilia?
What dangers would you invite

as a teenager to keep me awake
as the moon fades into a mo(u)rning

sky? Would we fight often, because
we'd be as singular and as alike

as a Queen Bee? If I could hold you
in my womb, I would shape my life

around you – like how a candle when lit
melts and moulds around something

close and tangible.

Stillborn

Jude Aquilina

After the stillbirth, someone has to make the phone calls
to stop the phone ringing with questions of 'boy or girl?'
Someone has to write to the old aunt who sent
the card and cheque, and return the borrowed cot
to the next-door neighbour.

Someone has to bundle up the booties and matinee jackets
and deposit them, like a dead pet, into the jaws
of a charity bin. Someone has to fold the crochet rugs
and pull the knitting needles from the row of woollen loops;
to paint over the frieze of teddy bears.

After the stillbirth, someone visits again and sits
with a cup of tea talking to the parents in a fug of unsaid words.
Maternity leave cancelled, she must sit on the bus again
looking out the window at the people and prams.

There is nothing to fill this small, unnamed space.
The burning of a lullaby catches in the ear; the snippet
of a nursery rhyme on a TV advert; the recess-time voices
from the nearby school. The calendar date, unmarked
but there every year like a frostbite.

New friends will smile, unaware. A girl will ask
if you'd like to nurse her new baby. And the years
will roll on like a coloured ball
but grief's ulcer never completely heals.

The Final Deaths

Julie Egan

A nurse beckons us to the quiet end of a corridor. 'It's probably time to start the morphine now,' she says. 'You realise that this is the end'.

We had the formal discussions with the doctors months ago. No artificial feeding. No treatment if he gets pneumonia. Now we have entered the final phase of a long dying. Instead of being overwhelmed by sadness, we feel a calm and solemn relief. Most of our grieving has been done already.

We are waiting. I had always imagined such a vigil to be grave and sad, relatives speaking in hushed tones, but we chat and read and laugh. We do the crosswords. The nurses bring us endless cups of tea and sandwiches. We go out to get consoling junk food and the bed tray fills up with pizza boxes and wrappings from fish and chips and half-drunk cups of tea. By the fourth day, my sister and I are at home here, going into the staff kitchen and making the tea ourselves.

Five days is a long time to watch someone die. We ask the nurses how long it will be. How will we know that death is approaching? 'Sssh,' they whisper. 'Hearing is the last sense to go.'

I first realised my father was ill when he started to neglect his garden. His pride and joy were the peony plants that he had inherited from his father. The large pink flowers bloomed in spring and every day he would check to see which one was ready to be picked.

I watched my father's personality and memories disintegrate as the tangled snarls and gaping holes of Alzheimer's disease ravaged his brain. The fragile coincidences of chemistry and electricity, the flickering patterns that formed tenuous webs or steely nets of memory—swimming in the Yarra, the men who came to the backdoor for a feed during the Depression, the cow his family kept on a block next to the house, his mother's early death from an infected finger in the pre-penicillin days— all gone. Now I am relying on that same molecular dance to tell you this story.

Dad dies early on Sunday evening. His breathing becomes ragged, a flurry of gasps, a silence and then a final breath.

We say goodbye but it feels hollow. There have already been so many departures, so many larger and smaller deaths. The Dad who sang tuneless Irish songs to my children, made speeches at family celebrations, ran marathons, took us to the footy even when it was raining, all those Dads gradually died. This is one of the deaths and not the most heart-wrenching. For a time, the individual cells will keep busily producing energy, making proteins, sending out signals, but soon each of them will die from lack of oxygen. The final deaths.

Outside, it is a beautiful spring evening. Dad's peonies are blooming abundantly and we will use them to decorate the coffin.

Dutchmans Beach

Carolyn Eldridge-Alfonzetti

It became a rite each holiday
to scratch the year in warm white sand
with a sun-bleached stick

Pink shoulder to pink shoulder
we'd bunch behind it
wearing swimmers and squinting
to smile for the camera—
net another memory

Last year
we drove you the short walk to the beach
held your elbows as you took
unsteady steps to the lace edge
where your children splashed silver
before the dying sun

This year
you hardly left the beach house
pillows propping your lolling head
and ravaged neurons rendering impossible
even the swatting of a fly

and we scribed the year on Dutchmans Beach
like numbers on a headstone

then huddled
and smiled just a little too broadly
beneath low grey bellies
of menacing clouds

Sail

Willo Drummond

In an instant you are a sail
loosed, flapping. Sprayed

with a sea of tiny blades —
a vast, over-sensate skin. Your silent

voice, a gaping mouth, calls
from a crack in the world: *desolate*

wind, sweep my knowledge
into oblivion, drop me back

in the well; all that sounds is the clink of flailing
shackles against the mast.

Experience says, in time,
the canvas will snap

taut. Right now
this sheet is the shape of living.

The ladder's blown
the world's all wailing wind.

Notes
'Crack in the world', 'wailing', 'wind': Selected Letters of Rainer Maria Rilke 1902 -1926 (trans.,
R.F.C. Hull, 1946: 173); 'desolate', 'wind', 'sweep my knowledge', 'into oblivion', 'drop me back in the
well': Denise Levertov, "Desolate Light," from Candles in Babylon, 1982.

Old Bones

Hazel Flynn

There is shuffling in the corridors, but it's not that sort of rehab.
No young things here, seeking sobriety. Ours are old bones,
ground down by life and replaced in a one-for-one deal.
The wonders of modern medicine, eh? we say,
learning to move anew on titanium, porcelain and plastic.
But the walking-wounded-by-design aren't the only patients here.

This little hospital, tucked away in the escarpment bush, also serves those
on their way out of this life. Usually, they are folded
in its innermost embrace, far from the well-appointed rooms
whose occupants are here by choice: *Like a holiday, almost.*
But sometimes such delicacy is not possible.
All the other beds are full, all the other options exhausted.

And so, last night, as I rested in comfort,
next door a man lay dying.
At first I thought his cries were from pain.
In the long hours before dawn, he moaned strange syllables,
Subsiding then building, loud then louder, again and again.
Cared for, but already far beyond help.

Never had I heard such noises, but their meaning could not be mistaken.
I'd long scorned 'passing on' and 'passing away'. *Just call it what it is, dying.*
Yet what I heard was a passage,
someone travelling one way: into the unknown.
Those formless cries were the body being forced to learn
how not to be. How to give up the ghost.

The sky lightened. Magpies began patrolling and carolling,
their sweet notes overlaying the breakfast trolley rattle.
My neighbour's soughing subsided,
then stopped for good.
Nurses passed by, murmuring.
Sheets were changed, forms filled out. A file closed.

Now the morning's new arrivals wheel in,
sore but not sorry,
brimming with plans.
So much they might do
with their new
lease on life.

Tsunami

Linda Harding

I sat in a church in Colombo, a few weeks after the tsunami hit Sri Lanka. I listened to a young woman tell of rising, as normal, on a Sunday morning, going out to feed the dogs, and hearing the sound of people running in the lane next to the house. Just running, no shouts. At that instant she was submerged in a massive surge of water.

When she broke the surface, she found herself being beaten by debris picked up by the never-ending, ever-crushing wave. She heard and saw terrible things in the next hours. Clutching some piping and doing her best to dodge huge pieces of buildings, trees, vehicles, she heard the voices of the dying, screams of agony. She swept past dead bodies. The force of the brown flood, reeking of petrol and sulphides and death, eventually eased a little and she was able to swim into a building, staggering up some stairs to get out of the water. On the second floor, she discovered a group of people: filthy, battered, bleeding, none of them able to speak let alone label what had happened. They were all tsunami survivors. Rescue finally arrived, but the young woman shook and cried as she spoke that day in Colombo. The wave had stopped but the trauma had not; that needed time.

Emotional losses can be tsunamis. They can pick us up and dump us raw and haemorrhaging on the edge of whatever comes next. By their very nature these tsunamis do not announce their approach. They hit us full force.

I watched my son be hit by a tsunami. His partner of four years left him quite suddenly, and it was weeks before the full wave of grief overwhelmed him. We were away at the time and returned to find him shaking, sobbing and somewhat incoherent. It was agony to watch. We did what we could to help: doctor, psychologist, even chicken soup. It felt like applying a Band-Aid after a heart had been ripped out of a chest. Watching from the sidelines was agonising. We wanted to say something but we didn't have the words. Yet our own journey with grief told us words are never enough, and often too much. Hugs are better, listening is vital, time is the friend you know will help the most.

The redemptive side of these cataclysmic floods is the opportunity they bring to reflect before we move forward. If we were only slightly drowned, we may have been able to continue along our original trajectory. But submerged to this degree, we have no option but to re-evaluate everything as we surface.

The young girl in Colombo found faith and friendship were her future. Our son healed and found new possibilities. The waters recede, and when they do, there's a chance to clean up and rebuild, even amidst the rubble of our traumatic memories. There is hope after the flood. So, hold on, breathe, wait.

All the Things You Didn't Know
Avril Mulligan

'It will take two years,' she said, divorced and still a little raw. 'About two years before you are on your feet again.'

You, in your naiveté, still in the first protective adrenaline rush of leaving, replied, 'Two years? It's not going to take me two years.'

You didn't know. You didn't know anything yet about uncertain futures and the stigma of a broken home. About not enough money and the loneliness of lost friendships, or the desperation of middle-aged dating. And you most certainly, as you gave your confident reply, did not know about holding the weight of your children's grief, as you hid yours from them.

You didn't know yet that endings could be so heavy; that they could press you to the bed unable to get up, or make you drop to your knees on the front lawn of your family home, the one you had left, the one you had just delivered your children to, where warm family life continued without you. Where your children were happy but you were now out in the cold, under the stars, not understanding why you couldn't seem to get up again and into the car, to call a friend, the only friend you could call in that moment of not being able to breathe and not knowing if you could walk away from this and certainly not knowing how you would get yourself back to your bare rental, family-less.

You did not know that it would take a long time, slow days and weeks and months. In fact it would take something pretty close to two years, because you would turn out to be just like everybody else after all. You would see that grief has no fast forward button, no way to skip through the stages; only the living of each day until they become easier. And you would tell this to your sister, when it was her turn, and the words would help her a little, but not take away the fact that she had her own days to live through, that were hers alone. In those early days, you did not yet know that grief is a desert, a place to walk alone, and a place that is not yet ready for new growth.

But there was another thing you did not know. For on the other side of the desert something was waiting. For when you were ready; for when it was time.

A place that fit, that felt right; somewhere you could grow and flourish.

Where new shoots of green would become the beginnings of a brand new garden.

And that when you arrived there, you would understand at last; this was why you had left.

Almost a Flower Vase

Philippa Armstrong

In 1980 we wore high-waisted cords, yours
   the palest blue, mine chocolate brown, our zips
zipped, our lips sticky with strawberry bonnie bell.

In '81 it was green eyes, grey eyes and best friends forever:
   you said *she's apples* meant we'd always be. And sand
and hair stuck fast with strawberry bonnie bell.

In '87 you gave me the cocktail shaker your grandma
   had given you, and, still, it smells of 1980 and an older
taint of Crème de Menthe, and, still, it smells of a cat-piss

hippie shop in Swanston St. On dark and smoky nights
   we descended the stairs to a spiritual sky and musky boys
when we snuck out—your fury and my hand-wringing

and our lips slicked with strawberry bonnie bell. And you
   ended you on Good Friday '88, your anger sovereign,
your self-hate jangling like piano keys, and you dangled

and crashed alone and far away in the cold morning.
   The strong jaws of a mechanical arm shook the thunder
of you and shook you and emptied you out like a wheelie bin.

Wordle for the Newly Bereaved

David Terelinck

You start out **ALONE**, before the last
of the mourners leave. Even long before,
when the oncologist tried to palliate
the impact of his words
at that final consultation.
How could you let your feelings flow
when you had to be his anchor?
In the togetherness of his dying,
you'd never been more alone.

Then you started to **AVOID** others;
politely declined at first. Eventually,
you stopped responding to invitations.
Finally, they didn't come at all.
No missed calls. No voicemail.

How **QUIET** it is now; just the memory of
condolences, the clink of cups and plates,
the whisper from black and navy blue.
And now that vacuum echoes with
his cheyne-stoke respirations.
But you dare not listen to the radio
just in case they play your song.

WIDOW isn't a big enough word
when you have to halve your life.
It should contain an 'N'
as you strain to peer beyond the pane
into a world without him.
And there are no words for
having to remember one scoop,
not two, and only half-filling the pot.
Still, you are grateful for lost appetites
in the overwhelming absence
of recipes for one.

Garden Song

Jessica Wallace

The almond is blossoming. Its flowers are early. They float in empty branches, high up and ethereal. The orange is still in fruit. Bright globes cling on as the season turns. Knotted grapevines hang from the weathered pergola. Under the Hills Hoist, the grass is a forest. A feral cat lazes among the soursobs. The neighbour's chooks fossick in the thick of it. They have free rein of the garden, as usual.

Inside the house is a hospital bed. Its mattress cover is plastic. Slippery and waterproof. Cotton sheets are spread, and a padded overlay is fitted, protecting the sheets from the body fluids that will stain them. The bed is huge. Industrial.

He says it's uncomfortable, but he doesn't want it changed. He's tired. Too tired to move. There is a pump at the foot of the bed. It groans to inflate his mattress when the air underneath him lessens. The sound of it disrupts the peace he has come home for. A pillow is strapped around it to muffle the noise.

The house is large and rundown, halved inside by a corridor that's heaving with furniture and shelves full of books. Rooms hoard storage: his mother's bedroom suite, the faux-walnut bedhead with matching wardrobe and cabinets, bags of clothing, pillows, blankets, mirrors.

Gleaned artworks hang elsewhere—small paintings and prints in the lounge room and kitchen. Exquisite ceramics, glazed egg-shell blue, and odd ornaments—a wooden monkey, a paper bird—are carefully positioned on the oak sideboard he'd restored. Guitars, records and songbooks everywhere. All gathering dust.

His room is modest. The bed is by the window, which he wants kept open. Cold air spills in. He smells the garden, the citrus and the blossoms. Listens to the trees creaking and the owl in the night. He remembers how the garden used to be, once upon a time, when his father was a young, driven man, planting seeds from the homeland. He cries for his mother— oh, how she'd cared for him. How she'd adored him and gave to him her dark, dancing eyes. He remembers his promise to return to his nonna, and to bring her sweets.

Friends bring him lavender. Rose oil and oranges. A bunch of parsley. A mandarin from his garden is peeled close to his nose, so he can inhale its perfume, greedily, lovingly. He closes his eyes, drifts away. When he wakes he says, *I'm still here.* A miracle: to be alive.

One morning a friend arrives with his guitar and plays until his fingers are numb. Afterwards he comes to the kitchen where the heater is on. He thaws his hands. Struck by sadness. The kitchen smells of coffee. Containers of drugs and syringes and folders of paperwork cover the table.

Was it only last summer they'd gathered under the vines? Spoke of music and the uncertain nature of love. When they'd braved the subject of loss, ever present in the dying man's life, right alongside abundance.

Hope Amanda
Simone Field

Two lines. Here, then gone.

Succumbed. That was the word that the clean cut, white robed, kind eyed doctor had pronounced, his gaze fixed on a grainy screen and his hand on a wand hovering over my midsection.

'It seems to have succumbed around 8 weeks,' he said clearly but softly. 'You're nearly 12 weeks now, so you can choose whether you wait for it to happen, or you go under here.'

Sudden, immediate tears. My outside knew before my insides caught up. I'll never forget the words spoken that day in that small room, in that old building. The scene is indelibly etched in my mind, an unplanned photograph of a piercing moment in time.

Sudden, immense grief, unexpected, but expected all the same. There's an innate knowing that happens sometimes around things like these. On a subconscious level, I'd known. I'd felt a momentary, deep wrench in my soul a few weeks back. A real certainty that I wouldn't hold this one in my arms this side of eternity. But that is a thought that seems ludicrous at the time. The wanderings of a mind caught up in imagining unrealistic catastrophe — nothing more. Shrug it off. Until I can't.

It was a girl. We named her Hope Amanda. Our little girl.

'How are you?' asks my dear sister-in-law, when we're on a walk a while after. Her gentle, brown eyes look upon me with knowing and kindness as she asks. She asks, not inanely but truly to know me, to weigh my feelings as heard and important. To show me that I am not alone. I consider my answer.

'Directionless,' I reply.

My course had been set, my sails had been filled, my path mapped out. My direction had been known, as the boat of my life headed with purpose toward a projected date. But now. I bob around on an ocean of confusion and loss, unsure of my trajectory from here. Stuck in the thoughts of what was gone, what I would never now know.

Time marches on.

As my mind emerges slowly from a fog, I begin to wonder about the future. My boat bobs around. I wonder if my heart will ever know how to move on. My body performs the machinations of everyday life.

For a while I don't know how to move my heart forward. So, I float. Bobbing in the ocean, trailing my hand in the water, watching the sun rise and set, seeing the other boats sail past, watching the birds fly in circles above me.

I'm not sure when it happened, but one day I begin to awake. One moment at a time. One day at a time. One iota of hope after another begins to add up, carrying the promise that life will find a new rhythm, that I will let go, that trying again one day won't seem so scary.

7 months later. Two lines. Here, and arrived. Hi there, little boy. Rainbow.

The First Five Days

Jo Gardiner

At midnight, I'm dozing in my bed in Woodford.
On the cupboard, the mirror rings deep blue.

The door frame gleams. My shoes lie careless on the floor.
You sit at the end of my bed, one eye closed.

A breeze peels away clouds, leaves the moon stunned
and pale in the window. Your upturned face is moonlit.

I'm not surprised by your presence. Nor am I afraid.
You have been here every night since you died.

Between the moon and the night lies the ground where
you live. In the morning, I won't mention this, lest it fade.

On your birthday in May we stood around
your bed. Three days later you were dead. In those days

I raked each leaf that fell into damp piles.
Now I live ordinary hours. A silver gum

swims on blue water. Strands of sunlight fall through
leaves to the bottom of the pool—like sinking gold.

Where I stand by the dusky moorhen and the rain lilies,
listening to the voice of the currawong, you walk too.

On the road, I find a cicada's green wings. They lie side by side
waiting for someone to come along and try them on.

Under the tulipwood, the flutter-tongued rock sparrow
blown in from the Iberian Peninsula, pecks in cracks

and flicks the yellow patch on her breast towards me to catch
as she pauses in her search for fruit from the Manchurian pear.

In the evening, the moon floats in pink cloud flanked
by the deepening blue of twilight. It is right that you

come at night. For it is in the night I leave you linen
bags of gold dust gathered from my day. After the fifth

night though, your presence grows faint, much like the way
you left your body that May. I sat close with you until

at dawn it seemed you'd wandered away and were no
longer there. I am sorry when, too soon, our midnight

meetings end, and when I wake, I simply note that you
and the moon are both gone, and I turn back into sleep again.

Our Loss

Joe Dolce

The 2 am call to me from her husband, the dread of telling her mother the horrific news, the anxious drive to the Austin Hospital, still half-asleep, the long wait in the hospital parking lot with her sons and their partners (COVID rules), her mother finally allowed in, with the husband, the rest of us much later, watching her quietly lying on the hospital gurney, on a ventilator, unsure what to do, the necessary drive back home to await the brain specialist, the CT scan, the numbing drive back to the hospital, the gathering in the waiting room with her older sister, her older brother (whom we haven't spoken to in seven years, the embrace and emotional reconciliation), the crushing news that it was hopeless to operate (catastrophic brain bleed), the decision to turn off the machines, the nurse reading through organ donation forms, a final farewell to her and heartbreak of listening to her mother whispering close to her, as though she could hear, how much she loved her, the leaving her behind, the silent drive home, the knowledge life-support was turned off, the reality of loss hitting us over the next days, her mother, in the bath, weeping that she couldn't go on, the desperate embraces at night, the intermittent and interrupted sleeps, the planning of the funeral, at first, no idea how to proceed, the service to be held at Montsalvat Colony, the choosing of the cardboard coffin (her wish), the idea for her youngest son to paint it, his trepidation that he wasn't able (too much grief), his grandmother's encouragement and offer to work beside him, adding flowers, the unforeseen dental emergency requiring her to have antibiotics and rest, the decision to let her grandson complete the painting alone, his brilliant achievement, the drive to Montsalvat to inspect the venue, the preparations: catering, printed programs, live video feed, photographic slideshow, order of eulogies and social media invitations, the late morning drive on the day for the ceremony, her husband's uncertainty whether anyone would come, the hall filling with an endless stream of family and friends, the gaily painted coffin covered in freshly-cut flowers, the moving service, her sister, husband and two sons speaking through their weeping, the fine measured talk by the esteemed author (a last minute addition), the reading of May Swenson's *The Key to Everything*, her mother's wonderful stories and memories with her, her oldest son's wife's unexpected but memorable recitation from the daughter's final book, *The Road to Tralfamadore is Bathed in River Water*, the wheeling of the coffin out into the sunny courtyard, the guests writing short messages on the box, the utterly perfect day, the furious bellbirds chiming, her coffin stripped of flowers carried to the hearse and driven away, the tea, cut sandwiches and scones in the long hall, the emotional goodbyes, the long slow drive, back home, exhausted, the days upon days following with intermittent tears and joyful recollections, of the lost daughter, that never end.

Chelsea's Lullaby

Gavin Austin

Of course we knew this day would come. Yet, nothing
could prepare us. I stand, helpless. Stolen, she is taken
away in a tiny zippered bag.

Thrashing in a swell of despair, you try to breathe,
desperately gulping a lungful of oxygen. For months
you and he held hands over your growing belly.
A smile as he felt her kick or roll. We painted the nursery.

Unexpectedly swept from her protective sea, she rode
the waves of your pain. You held her in brief, exquisite
goodbye. Now you hold her tiny footprints, ink on card
in your hands. My inadequate words ebb and flow.

A clotted image of her: shrunken, blue, will live on.
Tenderly, you trace her footprints with a trembling
forefinger; lasting proof. Like Armstrong's on the moon?

> early frost
> the iris bud
> unopened

The Marriage Arch

Anne M Carson

We're in the barge together   drifting along a kind of canal
I'm facing where we've come from   in the rower's seat

He faces where we're heading   flinty-eyed   He sees them
before I do   sees them as we float under the archway

He tells me and we return   as you can in dreams without
effort or action   This time I notice the archway is garlanded

with bees and their hive   a beautiful semi-transparent web
slung between the two uprights of the arch   It's loose

swinging gently in the breeze   You can see the hexagonal
construction of the honeycomb   the most remarkable thing

I've ever seen   One part of the comb is particularly dense
dark   textured like embroidery with many bees clustered

in bouclé   Exquisite   but laced with danger   I stop
rowing   stalled by beauty and hazard woven so tightly together

Each time we pass under the arch   many bees are disturbed
and fly out   Agitation troubles the air   I can tell he's

worried they'll swarm   attack us   I am too   Inexplicably
we return   a third time under the arch   then worry galvanises

us and I begin rowing   I row hard as if chased by bees although
I can't see if they actually pursue us   The feeling of menace

mounts   I haul on the oars with all my brute strength   speed
us away from peril   I can do it   I'm strong enough to carry us

both   I don't know if the bees follow us but the possibility
strong-arms my rowing   He navigates so I don't crash into

the bank   We tear under the final arch   then I glide through
to the other side   alone (again)   in the time after his death.

Time To Go

Dave Clark

My phone rang. It was my youngest brother, Steve, calling.

Dad had died. A constant in my life, now departed. *I am fatherless.*

I drove to the hospital to be with family, around Dad's body. Steve and Mum shared that he died so peacefully they hadn't even noticed it happening. That was so unlike Dad, to leave anywhere quietly.

We hugged. Cried. Laughed. I lost track of the discussion, staring at Dad's body.

The hospital staff needed to move Dad to the morgue, to free up the room for the next dying person. *Clear the stage.* It was understandable, but felt rushed, inadequate time just to sit with Dad.

We slowly left the hospital ward, looking back at it through flooding eyes. It felt too simple, leaving Dad for the hospital staff to sort out. Guilt twinged in my ribs. We drove to our parents' place and ordered pizza. Relief and agony began to roll in. It started as a slowly rising river, then became a dagger, then a foggy bewilderment.

I walked in repetitive circles around the paved backyard of my parents' place as I talked to my wife on the phone. The shock made it feel like I was describing a distant event to her.

I padded over to the raised garden bed and touched the leaves of the tomato plant. *Dad was so good at growing them.* Without him, they'd probably wither and collapse. A fleeting thought: *I wonder if we'll be the same.*

I walked inside. Dinner had arrived. As I held a piece of pizza with trembling hands, I looked around. Some notes in Dad's handwriting were next to the laptop. Books he was reading rested on a coffee table, a bookmark three quarters of the way through one of them. The brown mechanical armchair, no longer needed to gently hoist him up. A jar of peanuts on the kitchen bench, a favourite snack of his. I saw a picture of Dad on their—*no, Mum's*—bookshelf. The dagger came back and twisted.

A few hours later, I began unfolding the sofa bed. It had felt reassuring to hang out with family, but now I needed to lie down, curl up and shut out a crumbling world.

As Steve got up to leave, he jangled the car keys in his hands and a memory rocked through me. Before going anywhere, Dad used to pace the hallway, jangling the car keys and our nerves with regular hints that 'it's time to go.' He would rev the Ford's engine while we finished getting dressed, as though he was gearing up for a Bathurst hot lap. He bubbled with urgency. Always idling, never off. Life was to be shaped and impacted.

This time though, heaven's keys were the ones jangling, the celestial chariot's engine revving.

For a man who hated waiting around, it was Dad's time to go.

Inhospitable Landscape

Ellen Shelley

Today you scan the pavement
                like a body waiting to be told
what is and isn't working.
                On the phone I hear your chords running
low on fuel. A voice-box almost gone.
                Lines of *I am dying*. Questions
that raise hairs on the back of my neck.
                When you visit, would you like to go
through my wardrobe? Years ago, I would have jumped at the chance
                but you would not have had reason
then, for someone to take the clothes off your back, that now no longer fit
                unresponsive tumours, the wrong type of hormones,
a life shined out of reserves. I park outside your house
                like a thief and count my guilty blessings.
Weeds are pushing up through cement like labour,
                unstoppable—

Those Stones

Andrew Lansdown

Set around the small fishless
but papyrus-sprouting pond,
four roughly-flat foot-sized stones
taken from my father's backyard
before his house was sold.

They have settled in place,
those stones, as if they always
belonged to me, as if they never
once belonged to another man
or took the weight of his tread.

Already the native violets
have cozied up to them,
resting their small green hands
on their rough-edged shoulders
as if they were long-time pals.

The lovely lush poolside violas …
Several even are waving
petite white-and-mauve pennants,
doing all in their power
to make them feel at home—

those stones, those stones
that once felt my father's footfall.

To The Shack

Ada Lester

Mountains that are watching with an ever-present eye. Lakes that emerge in the mountains—mirrors to the clear, cold sky. Rivers that cascade through quiet places, looking for the sea. Coastlines of roaring waves that scatter salt across the sand dunes. Forests that smell like sweet rotting earth, dark and damp, soft and fertile.

There is a pilgrimage to these places every Christmas and Good Friday. But for a different sort of religion—a faith in the faraway.

Men returned from the war needing stillness and solitude, with others needing distraction. They built themselves huts made with timber and tin—a place to rest after a day outdoors, where they could drop their anchors and come ashore.

The men tried to escape the violence they had seen, yet their own land was stained with bloodshed. The men hoped to forget this when they called a spot 'mine', but the mountains saw the truth in their long looming shadows.

The land was claimed not bought. Miners, lawyers, butchers, surveyors—they all took a bit. They built their shacks alongside each other, without fences or front doors.

The children played together and found strange sea creatures, and ferns perfect for fairyland. The mother held her baby by the shore and dipped his toes in the water. She watched them curl with the cold.

The place was a constant in an unfolding life. The orange-coloured rocks were loyal, steadfast in the shifting sands. The children grew up, went away and longed to come back.

But things changed a little, others a lot. The coast became more costly, so the neighbours sold their spot. They had to pay rates and they needed the money. It was bought by another family who built a bathroom and a second storey.

There were tourists coming and they needed somewhere to stay, so some felt resourceful and rented their place. It kept the walls warm and the breeze flowing through, and it gave them a little money too.

Then people bought shacks just to rent; there was wealth to be made.

They filled them with old books, knitted rugs and seashells—curated like a museum display. There would be no children, no pets, and no parties, so their shack sat lifeless like a toy too precious to play with.

Their grandchildren have come back: they are adults now. Their parents are dead and the place is used less. It is harder to wipe away the dust. Rats live in the cupboard and eat through the flour. The neighbours are new each week.

The grandchildren think about selling or knocking it down. They could build somewhere to live and commute to town. The land is worth lots and they should split the cost.

The place is still there, under the mountain and beside the sea. The breeze blows through a broken window, thick with dried kelp. The grandchildren go down, every second Christmas and on Good Friday, when the traffic is light.

Cold Seed

Belinda Calderone

you fell
too young
eyes unopened
wings folded   translucent frames

but the pulse of your organs still labours
beneath your purple, featherless breast

in the softness of my garden's waking sun
I gather you   warm and weightless
in careful hands and place you
in a makeshift nest

together   we wait for her

between a day's chores
—folding sheets
simmering soup
vacuuming carpets—
I return and return to you

each time, I see you   straining
pink mouth opening to the sky
a silent call

together   we are waiting

but the day fades   hour by hour
until evening stills
your shivering breath
and your small body
lies like a tender stone

under the light of my garden's watching moon
my hands dig in damp earth
and plant you in the dark

my cold seed   you will never grow
yet I wait for you
to bloom

In the Distance

Emilie Collyer

Roused from sleep into 2am
confusion and his clumsy footsteps.
   'I missed her call,' he said, waving

his phone as if it were all
just an administrative error. As if,
   had he answered right away, the words

his sister uttered would have been different.
The bed was not raft enough to float, we
   were sinking in her voice

so far away: *He's dead, he died,*
no prep or warning, here and now not,
   as he'd lived, his own rhythm and beat.

We lay through the remaining
night hours. Thousands of kilometres
   away she did the same. In the morning

she got busy arranging the business
of death. We could not jump
   in a car or on a plane to help.

Borders closed. We walked, past the
brick dark corner house, we think the man
   who lives there is also a cat.

One rain slick night he yowled at us,
we wondered if the umbrellas scared him,
   looking like giant birds gliding horizontal

strangely close to the ground.
Around the bend to the park, evening now,
   the sky shouted pink

and everyone was out taking photos
trying to put beauty into their pockets.
   In the distance, a three-legged dog,

Oh, is the first thought, *poor thing.*
But stop to look, how it bounds joyful,
   making its own arc through the winter light.

Who Were You?

Rebecca Payne

She imagines the grief of other people to be a thing of beauty: blazing hot, red against the sky, while her own grief is a hard, shrivelled, black thing. For how do you grieve when you struggle to forgive?

She dreams of him still, and in those dreams he is alive and he is always angry. Sometimes the dreams plunge her back into the misery of those dark years. She is shaken the next day, sick to her stomach. In others, she shouts at him that he is dead and she is free, and she wakes full of guilt.

She keeps busy: her grief does not have the luxury of time. It has had too much time already. There was no sudden death, no shock of the funeral, no enveloping sympathy and stabbing grief. Rather, the years of gradual loss as he slowly changed and disappeared.

And always the anger. His anger, separating her from the world. For the world understands peaceful deaths, preferably involving hands held, relatives gathered by bedsides, and affairs neatly sewn up. It does not understand bitter, painful deaths.

She cannot speak of the end. Cannot tell of his misdirected anger when he was unable to pee and could not understand why she could not help him. She is haunted by the skeletal face and pumped up legs that made walking impossible. By then it was unbearable for him, who had been so physical, so proud, to be seen by others.

So many things that cannot be said. She holds her tongue around his family, with their gift for avoiding uncomfortable things. Absent at the end, they have their own way of remembering that is so different to hers. But she must smile and remain silent for the children—for god knows they have suffered too much already and need their family.

She cannot grieve with them, for they do not grieve the same man or even the same events. And she cannot properly grieve, for who is she to grieve? She remembers the man with the light in his eyes and the bush in his soul, who found endless contentment from very little. But his memory is crowded out by the critical, abusive patient. She cannot reconcile the two, or think of the first without the intrusion of the second. Was the abusive patient there inside all along, waiting to be exposed by adversity?

She clings sometimes to the idea that mood swings and hormonal changes are not uncommon. But 'it wasn't him, it was the illness' feels like a comforting lie for the children.

But a part of her does know he wasn't always like that. Remembers how he put her first, how nobody else mattered for so many years. Remembers that first day when she got in his car and felt no need to speak, to entertain, no need to do or be anything. Just the simple contentment of like-minded souls and tired bodies at peace.

I Must Write

Ada Lester

I have let go of his hand to write this. His hand is cold like porcelain. It does not feel like his hand, which was always clammy and warming my own. Thick and blistered skin wrapped around my fingers. I have been tracing his veins, the map across his knuckles and into his wrist, like the rivers that run behind our house, but even they have gone dry.

I have let go of his hand because I must write now, otherwise I never will. I feel the pressure of describing this, each word feels important, and because of that I will not write about it at all. I have always been like that with diaries. I write about an afternoon with a grandchild, what we ate, what we saw, the endearing things they said. But I do not write about the things that I feel. I have learnt this about myself, and I take note of what is left out. These are the important bits.

I am sitting in a hospital room, listening to Pete moan. I used to say he snored like a dying man, but he is not sleeping, he is letting life go. In each unconstrained sigh, he is letting it all go. I can hear the knot inside of him being unpicked, and with each moan, I hear it all. I pat his cold hand and I say 'Well done, you're letting it all go.'

I am stuck now on what to write, because what do I write about a life. I feel self-consciousness overwhelm me, the stupidity of trying to contain someone in words.

I must write now before nostalgia fades his image to a vignette, softened around the edges.

We know each other so well, it is a strange thing to know another person that well. That is why he is so hard to write about. I know him too well, and in anything I write, I will see only one small part.

Index of Stories and Poems

161